THE SECRETS I KEEP

For all those who helped and believed in me.

Being fearless feels good...

Copyright and all rights reserved. K J Miller.

ISBN-978-1-326-03779-6

Intro.

It's almost like, just for a moment, the world stops spinning. Everything moves in slow motion around you. There is just silence. Silence and Him.
At no moment in time was it anything he said or did to make my life revolve this way, it was just him.
It was always him. He was my hurricane. I was stood in the eye. Spinning too fast, moving so quick, shining too bright.
I just... I couldn't walk away. How could I...? when he smiles at me, that dazzling, heart rendering grin... It melts me like a forgotten chocolate, left on the window sill on a beautiful summer day.
That's what he is to me.
The sun.
The moon.
The stars.
Everything is different now. It all makes more sense.
I was meant to lose my balance, meant to fall for him... I guess he knew that when he saw me...
He became my peaceful place to rest, my silent world to sing in... there is never anybody there- it's always just me and him.
I don't want for anything else...

Just the sound his breathing makes when he holds me close at night...
The feel of his eyelashes as they flutter against my cheek...
The softness of his kiss as he places them over my neck...
The gentle beat of his heart as it sings me to sleep...
I think that... I think that I knew it was impossible for a man to be created so perfectly, yet, if the devil can treat you the way I was treated... surely God can bless you all the same... Right...?
I think the most frightening part of feeling this way is the idea of losing them...
That one day they might leave.
He became all my senses... the air in my lungs....
It wouldn't be just losing him...

It would be losing all of me.

Chapter 1

"BELLE! Are you coming back off your break, or what?" Ellie yelled through the door. Her olive skin flushed pink and dark hair stuck to the side of her face. She looked really sweaty as she quickly disappeared. Pissed off with me as standard, story of my stupid life.

I was supposed to be back from my break ten minutes ago but I'd been too engrossed in a book that I'd completely lost track of time, again. Not like they're not used to it though, happens all the time. When you're a social recluse like me, the real world - what really should matter - doesn't. Its mind-numbingly boring, the real action is always found in a good romantic novel, where you can just sit, dream and completely lose yourself in the wonderful world that will never quite exist. However, once again, I've been torn away to deal with the delights of the crappy restaurant I so helplessly slave in five nights a week.

"Sorry Ellie, my bad," I replied as I chucked the book into my bag and grabbed my pen, quickly following behind her "Is it busy?"

"It's booming." she replied bluntly as she rushed off to continue serving. I was never really offended when people didn't want to talk to me, in fact, considering I never made an effort to talk to others, why should they talk to me? Since I was 11 and went through...what I went through. It wasn't like I hated people. Just disliked them... with a passion.

    I put myself into autopilot and began aimlessly running around serving tables, I hated my job. I worked in a large Italian restaurant opposite the river in sleepy Norwich, England. There was nothing in particular I disliked, however. The customers were nice, the staff were ok (at times) and the hours weren't all that bad. It's just, since I was little I always felt there was more for me, like God had bigger plans. Guess he just didn't know what they were yet. I didn't either...but I was sure as hell it wasn't this. I liked to think that God tests you, prepares you for challenges, between the ages of eleven and thirteen I think I past my test. Yet here I was - dead end job, not a single friend and a perverted boss who seriously needed a punch in the face.

    I felt like years had gone by before the tables were finally cleared of customers and the manager, a short, chubby and bald man called Steve, was finally locking the front doors for the night. He was sweating repulsively, making his cheeks look like little red cue balls, I wondered why, considering the fact he had sat on his ass in the manager's office doing nothing all night while the rest of us ran around doing all the hard graft. Perhaps it was the big black suit he was wearing attempting to look smart, however, the wrinkles on his shirt and the coffee stain on his purple tie didn't help him look all high and mighty, like he acted. This guy was a class 'A' prick. We all knew it too. If he ever hired any staff, they were always girls, if he ever did the rotas for the week, he would always put himself on with girls. He was creepy in a million different ways, the number one way being he would only ever talk to your chest, eye contact wasn't a thing he has ever mastered. As I was finishing up cleaning the last of the tables, I felt his sweaty presence behind me.

"Belle?" he asked, as his voice echoed around the silent restaurant, his voice always reminded me of bag-pipes, his words were what you heard first and his breathing droned quietly behind the din.

"Yes, sir?" I replied as I turned around to face him. A creepy silence lingered as his eyes explored my body. I was a curvy size ten, with (if I do say so myself) quite a good bust size, but feeling his eyes burn into me didn't make me feel confident at all. It made me feel dirty, how my father used to make me feel. Shockingly enough, when he came to issue my uniform the day I started work here, they only had my shirt in a size eight (yeah, sure) I never questioned him at the time but now it seems highly unlikely that was the truth. I quickly pulled my long dark hair around my shoulder's, letting it fall on my chest, covering his view.

"Good work tonight," *as if you'd know you lazy bastard* "Good tits too."

"W... What?!" I stuttered, shocked

"Tips...good tips tonight." he corrected as his faced flushed a deeper red, handing me over my share and waddling off, to find Ellie and creep her out I presume. Shuddering I stuffed the money into my pocket and quickly finished off the last table then headed round the back to see if she needed help with the kitchen.

I found her in pot-wash, laughing with Daniel, one of the chefs. Flirting disgracefully.

"Oh hey, Belle. You coming tomorrow?" she asked as I strolled up towards them.

"Coming where?"

"The Christmas party?" she stated, looking at me like I was dumb for not knowing, however, this was the first I had heard of it. And another thing - a Christmas party in the middle of November? Seriously?

"Oh...erm... I never received the invite." I fiddled with my apron, almost positive I didn't receive it because it was never sent "It's cool though, I probably wouldn't have come anyway so it would have been a waste of paper." I added, taking back the higher ground.

"Paper?" Ellie burst out laughing "Belle, you make me laugh."

"Why?" I asked, intrigued.

"It was on Facebook, a Facebook invite." her face straightened for a moment "You have Facebook, right?"

"Erm... no... not so much." I sucked in a breath feeling the awkward tension as Ellie gave Daniel the 'listen to the freak' eyes. "You need a hand here then? Or can I shoot?"

"Nah, got it. Cheers though." she replied, turning round to finish cleaning the sink, smirking as Daniel headed back to the kitchen, chuckling arrogantly.

"I'll take the rubbish out, then head off

then, if that's ok?" I asked.

"Yeah, sure. Later."

"Later." I responded as I hauled the black bag over my shoulder and headed up the long corridor towards the back entrance leading out to the dumpster. Pushing the fire exit open, the cold hit me, it was the middle of November and there was two inches of crisp, thick snow laying like a perfect blanket on the ground. *Great,* I thought to myself as I realized my little black sneakers were about to give way to the cold and wet, the idea of having to walk home in this wasn't filling me with joy either, and being almost one in the morning, it was pretty cold!

Staring at my footprints in the snow I slowly made my way over to the dumpsters and threw the heavy bin bag inside. *Phew.* Trying to step on the same footprints I made there, I slowly made my way back, that is until, in my periphery vision I saw a dark figure in the car park, just stood there.

"JESUS!" I yelled out loud in shock as the figure began to move away, I couldn't see any details but it looked like a man with a tall, lean figure and long coat, almost to the ground. I just stood there, frozen, as I watched him slowly walk away. I've lived by myself for three years now, and to be honest, I don't have a single person I'd call a friend, so I'm always on high alert. Never trusting anyone. Never needing anyone. Never wanting anyone. Especially not weirdos who stand in the middle of the car park at one in the morning in the pitch black.

    I rushed back into the building and straight into the staff room on the left. It was a tiny room consisting of one brown (slightly distressed) sofa, a coat rack and a mirror (Steve liked us to look good. Pervert) staring into it as I put my coat on, I examined my face. My mascara had all but worn off and my face looked pale and tired with my brown eyes looking like muddy puddles and my lips dry and colorless. Brilliant. *No reading tonight, straight to bed,* I promised myself although I knew it wouldn't happen. I pulled my long hair, which extended right to the bottom of my back in waves of auburn and chocolate, to the side and slid on my wool hat, then my gloves before taking off.

    The walk back to my flat was no more than five minutes away, a quick, easy walk which was mostly lit up by street lamps apart from a little alley way which took less than a minute to walk down. Pushing open the back door, I briefly scanned the parking lot to make sure the man had gone. He had. So with that, I set off on my journey home. Most of my journey home was uphill, so with the paths being icy I knew my walk was going to take double the time, and being the world's clumsiest fool, a slip on the ice was definitely on the cards. There was no noise outside, no cars on the road either, just the sound of a single crow occasionally filling the air with its calls. It was probably calling out for his lover, I decided. I guessed he had lost her during a flight somewhere. Or perhaps she had left him. Who knows. That was one of my flaws, I was a hopeless romantic. I blamed it on all the books I read, I loved books about angels, fallen angels who came down to find the women they loved, stupid I know, but I loved them. The chances of a romantic story happening to me was slim to none, considering no one could really get within five foot of me without me freaking out. So I had to settle for just reading about love, it was a definite second best.

  I was pulled out of my daydream to see the crow swoop down and land on the snow covered wall next to me, he tilted his head as his eyes just glared at me. I stopped walking and glared back

"Little creepy don't ya think, Mr. Crow?" I said with a little giggle, realizing I was talking to a bird. His loud squawk filled the air as I took a step backwards, that *was* creepy. It was then I heard footsteps behind me. Peering back, I saw a figure walking heavily towards me as my heart began to thud. I wondered briefly if it was the same man from the car park as his long coat was vaguely recognizable.

Who cares, Anabelle... Run, my subconscience ordered as I quickly starting walking, faster and faster as my feet slid on the snow. I felt tears well up as I contemplated what to do. Should I just stop walking and see if he walks past? Should I run and see if he does the same? I didn't own a mobile phone so a fake conversation to scare him was out of the question. I decided in my blind panic to cross the road, if he crosses too then I would run. The road was built up with old looking houses, none of which had their lights on, but I knew if I screamed someone had to hear me. Even though I was little in size and just twenty years old I knew my lungs wouldn't let me down, they were big enough to make a loud scream if I needed to. With that I crossed the road and made it safely to the other side quickly, still keeping my walk fast-paced. With a swift glance over my shoulder I noticed he had done the same.

Shit. Shit. Shit.

Cross back over, I thought again, he might just be going this way. By now his long legs gained a lot of distance between us and I was beginning to think it was time wasting. *'Fuck it'* I swore in my head as I darted back to the other side of the road again, this time not stopping my jog, trying to convince myself not to look behind, just to run. I couldn't stop my eyes from daring to peep behind once more and, sure enough, he had crossed back over to my side of the path as well. I felt my eyes burst into tears as I began to sprint forward, I heard his footsteps increase too. He would catch me, no doubt about that. Would he kill me? Who knows. What did he want? Who cares? Suddenly I felt my feet slide on the snow beneath me. Everything seemed to slow down as I closed my eyes, preparing to hit the floor. Preparing for him to catch up to me, prepared for him to kill me or whatever he was planning on doing. Preparing for the coldest of the snow to cause the first pain but... I didn't hit the floor.

I landed in someone's arms but panic still overcame me. I instantly spun my head and the man was still there, but no longer running. He just stood there, watching me. Slowly he spun round, turning on his heels. Watching his coat sweep round to follow him, he casually strolled off in the opposite direction. Struggling to control my breathing, I looked at my hands which were clung to someone's arm, I was shaking uncontrollably and tears still streamed down my face. Yet, I wasn't afraid. Someone's arms were wrapped around me, I was protected. I dared a look at my savior, the person who just literally appeared from nowhere, so it seemed. As my face moved upwards, my eyes met with the most striking face I had ever seen.

Chapter 2

"Are you OK?" his voice sung and it was like music, like a perfect love song in the mist of complete madness, my madness.

"I... Erm..." realizing I was still seeking comfort in his embrace I quickly took a step backwards as his arms fell to his side "Sorry." I whimpered again, unsure of how to explain why I just fell into him, and also unsure why clinging to him desperately didn't make me freak the hell out.

"Don't be" he replied as a beautiful smile crept onto his face, which the street lamp now lit up perfectly. His hair was shoulder length and a beautiful golden-brown color which shone and glistened with its streaks of auburn. His eyes were other worldly, golden to match his hair with chocolate rings circling them, like a caramel eclipse in a chocolate sky. They were framed with the most delicate lashes, black as the night. His jaw was strong and yet seemed gentle, shadowed with well-groomed stubble. I felt my eyes sweeping over him, admiring his dress sense. He was entirely in black from what I could see, black jeans, shiny black shoes and a warm, black duffle coat, fastened right to the top...and he was staring at me like I was an absolute freak for just standing there, glaring at him. *Say something, Belle!*

"I... Erm... didn't know him." I stuttered, fully aware that I probably made no sense to him, yet his warm smile appeared again, lightening the night.

"I see." sung his unspoiled voice once more "Where are you off to at this time of night?" he questioned.

"Home. I just finished work." I replied, feeling slightly feeble under his stare.

"Let me walk you there" he replied. I was still terrified over what had just happened, scared the creep in the long coat would come back if I was left alone again, but then, reality kicked in and I remembered I didn't know this man in front of me either. He could be anyone!

"Thank you, but I only live a few minutes away, I should be fine" I said, still unsure what the right thing to do in this situation was.

"More the reason for me to walk you there, it's not out of my way. *Please*" his eyes wore into me and I suddenly knew the right answer. This man saved me, he was safe. It seemed completely reasonable for him to walk me home.

"OK... Thank you" I replied, knowing my

flat was just down the dark alley way on the right, it would take just a minute or two.

"Lead the way," he said as his hand extended and I began walking "My name is Amadore Renato." he continued, strange name, Italian perhaps?

"Erm... I'm Anabelle... Anabelle Jones" I said as I slipped on more ice and gasped, ready to hit the cold floor. He quickly grabbed my arm, saving me yet again from a cold meeting with the ground. "Sorry, again." I added as I felt my face flush a deep pink as that gorgeous smile grew bigger with amusement. Biting my bottom lip, I straightened myself up before walking ahead. He followed, silently next to me. The small alley made it difficult for him to walk by my side so he dropped back as we walked through. A street lamp lit the end, leading the way to my studio flat which sat on the third floor of the tall building on the right. The whole journey, which took around two minutes, I spent trying with all my might not to slip anymore, but somehow, I knew I'd be caught if I did. I came to a stop outside the electronic door leading to my flat and began rummaging through my bag for my keys

"It was a pleasure to meet you tonight,

Anabelle." Amadore said as he closely examined me searching my bag "Everything alright?"

"I can't find my" I stopped as I pulled my keys out of my bag. "Bingo." I continued, relieved a trip back to work wasn't on the cards.

"You are very amusing to me Belle; may I call you that?" I didn't know whether that was a compliment or not. I'd just had a horrific experience, being chased by a really scary, tall man... and that was amusing to him?

"Yes, you may. However, I don't really see what you're finding amusing." I replied, feeling annoyed.

"Your eyes, you are charming to me." he responded as I felt my anger disintegrate. *Charming,* I thought to myself. I'm sure I'm staring into the eyes of the meaning of that word.

"Oh..." *think of something smart to say, God damn it Belle* "... Thanks."
Oh, well done!

"Hopefully we will meet again soon." he said as his grin lingered and his eyes stayed fixated on me.

"Hopefully." I said as I attempted some sort of nervous, goofy grin of my own.

"Perhaps you wouldn't mind if I walked you

to your door, to make sure you get into your flat safe? *Please*"

"Erm..." I would almost definitely say no to this sort of request, no one has ever seen the inside of my home, but for some reason, his caramel eyes stared deeply into me and his request seemed very rational. I had just been scared out of my mind, of course this man would like to make sure I'm safe. There was something about him which seemed very mysterious in that moment, I watched briefly as his eyes flicked towards the third story windows and his nostrils flared slightly. If I wasn't paying so much attention to his striking face I would have missed it, but I didn't. He was worried... and so was I. I hadn't once told him I lived on the top floor of the block of flats, yet, that's where his eyes kept getting distracted to. "Yes, please do." I finally responded as a grin swept over his face once more.

"Wonderful. After you, Belle." he replied as he held open to door. He took the stairway with ease and when we reached the top I was trying desperately to disguise my breathlessness.

"This is my one here, number seventeen." I said, panting somewhat. I watched intently as through his smile he examined the door. For the briefest of moments, I saw something in his eyes. Worry? Panic? I was unsure, but as quickly as it appeared, it disappeared. His beautiful face shone back at me.

"Goodnight, Belle. *Sleep well.*" he said as he took one step closer to me and stared deeply into my eyes "*Leave a window open.*" he added, before smiling and disappearing back down the stairs.

I heard what he said, I knew I had, but, for some crazy reason I didn't have a clue what it was. I decided he must have just said "goodbye". Shaking my head at my crazy insanity I slipped through my door and quickly locked it behind me. I flicked on the light and stared into my cold, lonely flat. '*Honey, I'm home*' I thought as I slipped off my hat, coat and gloves and chucked them onto my couch. Who was that weirdo that followed me? What did he want from me? I could have used a closer look at his face. Perhaps I should call the police?

My brain was so exhausted from the crazy night. I went straight into my bedroom, chucked on my 'Where's Wally' PJ's and tied my hair into a messy ponytail, *no reading* I promised myself as I opened my window, before slipping into bed and dipping into a deep, restful sleep.

Chapter 3

My bedroom was freezing cold when I finally opened my eyes and rolled over to look at the time. Eleven thirty. Great.

It was my day off today but I had so much to do, cleaning, shopping, beauty regiments and, of course, all of those things were going to be lucky if they got done as I had some serious reading to attend to.

I stretched out and rolled over, I felt like I had just dropped into a coma, my sleep had been so heavy and my dreams so vivid. Dreams of Amadore Renato, catching me as I slipped and fell, falling to a certain death, yet - there he was. His strong hand reaching out and saving me.

I sat up and rubbed my eyes, quickly leaping out of bed to close the window. I briefly wondered why I had opened it last night. Deciding not to waste time worrying about the crazy things I do when I'm tired, I headed to the bathroom to shower.

Once dressed in plain jeans, a grey sweater and tennis shoes, I examined myself in the mirror. My eyes looked brighter than usual and my freshly blow dried hair looked full of life and body,

I obviously needed that sleep. I turned round to grab my coat from where I had left it last night, deciding to do the shopping first as I was starving, only to find it was hanging neatly with my hat and scarf on the hooks on the front door. ...*hmmm...* I thought as I distinctly remembered throwing it all on the couch before I went straight to bed. *I must have hung it up,* I thought *stop being weird* I chastised myself as I grabbed them and headed out to the store.

Browsing the isles, I scrutinized my basket, so far full of snacks and fizzy drink, not good! I was so hungry that everything seemed appealing, nothing more than Amadore Renato though. His image lingered in my imagination as I desperately tried to forget about my dream and fill my basket with sensible items, like bread or pasta...anything but chocolate! I found myself grinning to myself as my imagination ran wild, creating scenarios that I played out in my head. *Seriously Anabelle, snap out of it!* my conscience reminded me

"Anabelle." I spun round as my breath quickly withdrew from me "How lovely to see you again." Amadore's voice rang just as beautifully as I remembered and his beautiful lips and brown eyes smiled contently at me.

"Erm... Hi", I replied awkwardly as I silently wished I wasn't so tongue-tied and inept, However, his crooked grin stayed where it was, lighting his features and radiating warmth.

"May I help with your basket?" he questioned without waiting for an answer, his eyes stayed locked on mine as he gently took the basket from my hand. I felt under some sort of spell as I released my hand, allowing him to carry the weight of the junk food I had acquired.

"Thank you." I said as secret butterflies fluttered in my belly. I felt a smile creep across my face, an embarrassing girly crush smile, one that came equipped with rosy cheeks and some sort of high pitch giggle. Oh dear - the shame!

"You always appear when I'm... hmm... free as a bird, Miss Jones." I noticed his stutter, he had to think of his words too. I wondered if he was as nervous as me and quickly decided he wasn't. "May I help you with your shopping?" I felt an urge inside me that I had never felt before, I wanted him to stay and help, I wanted his company.

"You may, Thank you." I grinned and looked away, hiding my eyes under my eyelashes for a brief moment before scanning the shelves for something to add to my basket, grabbing some peach squash and handing it to him I felt my butterflies tremble some more.

"So, last night Anabelle, had you seen that man before?" he questioned. As I recalled the events which were still raw within me, feeling fear rise like bile in my throat, I quickly snatched a bag of dry pasta off the shelf and put it straight into the basket.

"I have never seen him before, no. He just followed me...from work." I replied, choking on my words as I tried to appear less scared than I was.

"Did you call the police?" he questioned again, seeming as composed as I was trying to be.

"No... it was nothing." I lied as I evoked the incident again, this time noticing my hands beginning to shake, I had to change the subject.

"You're right, *forget it, Anabelle, it was nothing.*" and with that, I did. I had completely forgotten what we were talking about, I blushed and looked at him, worried he was waiting on an answer that I didn't have, he was just smiling at me so I grinned back and flushed a deep red.

"Erm...." I stuttered "What did you say?" I asked, hoping I didn't sound too crazy

"I said that you look beautiful today, Anabelle." His compliment sent my butterflies into some sort of frenzy as an awkward chuckle, which sounded similar to a horse having a seizure, escaped my lips, so shameful!

"I... Erm... you look... Erm... great, too." *How embarrassing! Just shut up Belle!* I chastised myself, annoyed I wasn't that confident, outgoing girl I had always wanted to be. Instead, I was an awkward loner that couldn't even talk to a handsome guy without blushing and stuttering like an outcast of society. He must think I'm such a tool.

"Why, thank you, Belle. It must be the coat, it's new." he said with a grin as my mind replied with *nope, it's just you!* Not allowing that response to exit my mouth I went with "Must be that then, it's a nice coat." Biting down on my bottom lip I glanced to the floor, letting my hair fall from behind my ears and shelter my face from his heavenly stare for a moment. He brushed down his sleeve and picked off a piece of lint, seemingly proud of his new black duffle coat, I took in how smart he looked again. Like last night, dark blue jeans, smart black shoes and a smile that could melt the arctic.

We went round the last few isles in silence. He followed behind me, as I reached for items to put into my basket his hand would appear to add them himself. I muttered a shy "Thank you." every time. He waited beside me as I paid for my three bags of groceries. All the time my senses were so aware that he was there. My hairs stood up on end as he shifted closer to swiftly take the bags and waited as I shoved my purse into my pocket.

"You don't have to...I mean, I can take them, if you want." I said, feeling slightly bad that he was just minding his own business and now he is lugging my heavy shopping around.

"No, please, I would like to carry them, unless you're trying to get rid of me, Belle?"

"I'm most certainly not trying to do that; I just feel bad."

"Well, please don't. I like being around you." His reply sent shivers shooting up my spine and exploding in my brain, like he had lit a beautiful firework inside me.

"I like being around you too," I replied as I cursed myself for being too open with him. I still didn't know him at all, although I wanted to, believe me!

"That makes me very happy," a stunning

grin lit his face. It was luminous and beautiful and caught me completely off guard "May I walk you home again?" he asked as I attempted a casual response

"Please do." I grinned and held his gaze for a moment. He adjusted the shopping bags so he held them all with one hand and raised the other hand.

"This one is for catching you, still icy out there." I bit my lip and my blush grew a few shades darker.

"Right... Thanks" I mumbled as he chuckled, his angelic laugh bringing my own smile to my face "Glad I amuse you, Mr. Renato." I added as we exited the store and began the short walk back to my flat.

"Amuse me? Understatement of the century." he said as his hair blew over his face, hiding the smile I was so desperate to see. I thought for a minute about what he meant, perhaps I wasn't just amusing... perhaps I was some sort of sideshow freak to him, or a circus clown that everyone laughs at when they fall. My thoughts hurt me. "Oh, no. I didn't mean it like that, Belle," he responded quickly to my obvious self-esteem issues, disguising what seemed like an inner kick to himself "You... Captivate me." he recovered as my self-hatred turned into embarrassment. There is no way in hell he was real.

    I continued to walk as he followed, I thought I heard him cuss under his breath, although I wasn't sure so I ignored it.

    "I've never seen you around here before, Amadore. Now twice in two days. Are you new around here?" I questioned to break what seemed like a long silence.

    "Yes, I came over with my brothers last month," he said as I slid once more, he caught my arm and grinned "from Italy."

    "Oh, nice." was the only response I could muster as the heat from his hand gripped my arm. When he released me it lingered there, strong and warm. I hoped it would remain there longer than it did. "You don't have an accent though... are you Italian?" I queried, trying to move past the embarrassment quickly.

    "My name is... and I was born there, but I travel a lot. I was only there for a short while recently."

    We trudged on through the snow, chatting aimlessly about how crappy snow was and how it was a 'danger hazard' (his words). His eyes always staying light and amused... captivated perhaps. I had no idea why. We got to my apartment block and I buzzed us in, assuming he would walk me to the door. He did, of course. Fighting my way up the steps and hiding my exhaustion, I fiddled with my keys, pretending not to notice how quickly and easily he could take them, his breathing hadn't sped once when we reached my door.

"Thanks again..." I said as I held my hands out to take my shopping. Then he took my gaze.

"I'll help you put it away, if you like? *I'm no threat to you, Belle.*" I thought quickly about letting him come inside, no one had ever seen inside my flat, apart from my mother when she helped me move in, before she fluttered off back to her millionaire lover-toy boy. I didn't know if I was capable of letting him in... but - for some reason - I knew he wasn't going to hurt me. *What's the harm?* I convinced myself *let the sexy man in!*

"Okay, come in." I whispered as my conscience kicked in. WHAT THE HELL she screamed... but before I could chastise myself further he was inside, placing the heavy shopping on the kitchen side. I stood nervously, unsure of how to act and what to say to the company inside my home. Knowing you're supposed to offer tea, or have conversation or something... anything. However, I was quickly reminded of how much I suck at being sociable as I looked down at my feet, which were apparently glued to the floor. Amadore slid closer to me, his breath hitched as he leaned around me, closing the door behind me and stepping back.

"You're letting the heat out." he said, almost trying to explain the closeness "Hey, you OK?"

"I... Erm..." I stuttered some more, unsure if I was okay or not. I hadn't been alone and ordered to make conversation since... since I was eleven. Since my father, Bill, made me talk... and do other things to him. At thirteen, when my mother found out, it was too late. I've been a recluse ever since. Unable to bond with anyone on any level. Now, here I am, making small talk with a man, admittedly a heavenly man. Well, trying to make small talk. As I said before, I suck at this.

"Do you want me to go?" he questioned further.

Yes "No." *damn it, Belle.*

"Are you going to come in?" he asked, confusion sprayed across his face. I was being a total weirdo; I knew it too. I bet he is wishing I said yes to him leaving, so he could run for the hills away from me.

"Erm... come in? ah... yes." I said, as I walked over to the kitchen area on the right, forcing my heavy feet to move with me. "Am I supposed to offer tea?" *Fuck it!* "I mean; do you want a cup of tea?" I bit the inside of my cheek hard, something I haven't done for a while, a trait I'd managed to dispose of when I moved away from everything, at seventeen.

His fingers were instantly on my face, brushing my cheek lightly as pain spread over his eyes, and fear struck in mine.

I slapped his hand away and fell backwards into the kitchen side as my groceries flew across the floor, losing my footing as I tumbled backwards. Grasping at the kitchen side but failing to do so I almost hit the floor, but of course, he caught me, staring straight into my eyes

"*Calm down... Calm, Anabelle...* I apologize, that was incredibly stupid of me. It won't happen again.... I'm going to stand you up now, remain calm. *You make the tea...* I'll pick up the groceries... *No big deal, OK?*" I was under a spell, I knew it too, his caramel eyes glistened as I heard every word, he made utter sense, it was no big deal. That was apparent... no big deal.

He stood me up as I straightened my shirt, feeling calmness spread over me, smearing my rough edges with his delicious, honeycomb voice. I began on the hot drinks.

"Sugar?"

"None for me, thank you, Belle." he replied as I turned to face him from the kettle. The shopping was already tidied and he was putting the new carton of milk in the fridge and passing me the opened one.

"Thanks." I said calmly as I poured it into our cups and handed it back.

"Where does the pasta go?" he asked breezily as my mind fought to remember what just happened. Something did, I knew it. This is not normal for me, perhaps it's him, his presence just calms me... was that even possible? For me to be friends with someone?

"What just happened?" I said, risking sounding a complete nut-job.

"Nothing, it was no big deal... stop fighting it." His eyes bore into me hard, I felt him in waves flooding over me *'fight it'* my conscience yelled as I slammed my eyes closed, I pleaded with myself to listen to the words "Okay, you want to play it this way." he carried on as my eyes opened to meet his frustrated gaze "You fell over, again, I caught you though... No big deal." I recalled what happened, how embarrassing. I had stumbled backwards. My cheeks got warmer from discomfiture as I let out a puff of air and rolled my eyes at myself. I could see it now... I would form a relationship with the heavenly man, based on the fact that he probably couldn't bare the idea of me being alone. I was a giant, walking accident waiting to happen. Just waiting to slip over and break my neck. Brilliant.

"Oh, yeah... sorry." I muttered

"Don't worry about it, shall we sit?" he replied, changing the subject as I took a moment to take him in. He was taking off his coat as I admired the view. His dark blue jeans fitting him perfectly, topped off with a neat black polished belt. His shoes were smart and his copper shaded sweater complemented his skin tones, showing off his collar bone and how stunningly sexy he must be under his clothes. Just the inches around his neck and collar told me he was toned and chiseled. His hair hung loose around his shoulders, shimmering in tones of chocolate and caramel, matching his eyes, which I finally noticed, were watching me too.

"Sit? Yes. Let's sit." I turned around and grabbed the mugs handing one to him, he took his without breaking eye contact, smiling contently all the while. I watched as he waited for me, he seemed nervous around me too. Watching, waiting, sizing me up and figuring me out. '*Good luck with that one*' I thought. I moved towards the couch and he quickly settled on the rug on the floor, for that I was slightly glad, distance would help me remain calm... I hoped!

"A day off today then, Miss Jones?" he asked, amusement once again stealing his face, replacing the confusion that was there before.

"Yes, off today. You?" I asked, aware I had no idea what he did for a living, then suddenly realizing I knew nothing about him at all.

"Yes, me too." he thought for a moment "Well, I work when I want to." he continued then waited for my next question, his eyes giving him away, he was enjoying this. I had no idea why.

"What does that mean?" I asked because he expected me to.

"I work in security," he stated and I felt I should ask more, but I left it, sensing he did not want me to.

"Cool…" I sipped on my tea, blowing it afterwards as the heat scolded my tongue.

"What are you doing tonight?" he asked with intent.

"Reading, probably. You?" my thoughts kept continuously reminding myself that I didn't know this man, but my sub-conscience kept urging me forward. I wanted to know him, all of him.

"Hopefully, taking you out… if you'll let me?" He stared at me, his eyes scorching through me, I felt him pull me apart, stripping me down. A situation I would, in most cases, panic. But I didn't. He was no threat to me. I didn't know why I knew this. But I knew.

"Why?" I asked.

"Why what? Why would you let me?" he replied, confused again.

"Why would you want to?" I clarified, feeling pathetic and feeble.

"Because I want to know you, Anabelle." his response was to the point, and it warmed me to the core, heating me deep inside. I'd been desperately lonely for nine years; I knew the most part of me was ready for someone to just talk to. Could it be a man though? An elegantly angelic man?

"Where?" I asked again, already knowing what my answer was going to be, knowing to well, he knew also.

"A bar? Or for a walk? Or my place? Anywhere you like." It seemed that reply from any other guy would sound desperate, I knew that to any other guy I would have rejected the idea immediately. But from him, all the suggestions seemed appealing, inviting.

"OK." I replied as his heavenly grin swept over his face, making my breath hitch.

"Okay. Good. I'll pick you up at seven." he responded as he rose from the floor, and strolled over to the sink to rinse out his mug. His walk had an animalistic, predator way about it, he walked with purpose, like he owned the room.

"Amadore... I don't usually... Erm," I couldn't find the words, I wanted to be honest with him, yet I was unsure if I was capable of it "... Socialize." I managed, as shame and embarrassment flooded over me. I felt his presence close to me as I looked up. He'd walked back over to the sofa and was crouched in front of me, he looked into the space between us, keeping it just enough that I didn't feel the need to move.

"Don't usually...? But you are prepared

to?" he asked as his eyes glistened and looked into me again.

"I... I think so... I can try." I stuttered feeling delicate... and a fool.

"Good, I'll take you home whenever you want. You'll be safe with me, Anabelle." He offered me a genuine smile and I returned it with one of my own, widening his.

"Seven O'clock then." I said as I swung my legs off the couch where I had had them, into his personal space. I don't know why I did it, as we were instantly very close, I felt strange, being so close to another person, my breathing sped as I decided that I had pushed my luck, that I wanted to be near him, yet I knew I was incapable. I pushed forward on the gap between us anyway. Bringing him closer, punishing myself. He withdrew quickly, standing and stepping back as I stood up. To anyone watching, the ordeal would have seemed completely normal, but the tornado inside me said otherwise, I got a little calmer as he turned and walked to the door.

"Seven." he grinned as he let himself out.

Chapter 4

I spent the rest of the afternoon showering, getting ready. Doing my hair and make-up and trying on every item of clothing I owned, settling on my skinny jeans, a black fitted vest and my black sneakers. Casual yet cool, I decided. I tried reading, twice, but my thoughts kept getting owned by Amadore. I sat on the couch, staring at the floor where he sat, twiddling my long dark hair, which I had left in waves flowing down my back. There was something else to him, I knew this all too well. I wondered if he noticed that about me. If he could sense I was damaged and perhaps not worth his time. I battled my thoughts most of the day, my thoughts telling me that this was some sort of joke, that he was not real. The most part of me knew he wasn't going to show up at seven. Why would he? But when my door sounded at seven pm exactly I was excited and nervous. Confused yet happy. I buzzed him in through the intercom and gathered my things together before he knocked at the door. I rushed over and answered it, taken back but how utterly gorgeous he looked, like he'd been sent down from heaven, ready to save me, to save my life.

"Good evening, Miss Jones." he breathed as he stole a look over me, I felt pathetic under his gaze, I knew I didn't deserve eyes like his on me. They were too perfect to waste their time and I was too ugly inside. But he was here, why would I let him go, he'll leave when he realizes who I really am, until then I decided to enjoy it while it lasted... if I could.

"Hi..." I breathed back "You look nice." I offered as I took him in, he'd changed as well, into smart black trousers and a chocolate brown shirt, fitted perfectly around his abs, showcasing his perfect body. His smart black shoes and trademark black duffle coat completed his look, making him look utterly divine.

"You look... really nice, too." he offered, pausing in-between. I knew he was fibbing, I had nothing compared to him, but I accepted the compliment, like he would have wanted.

"Thank you." I replied "Where to?"

"You eaten?" he questioned as I quickly remembered I hadn't, I'd spent the afternoon fantasizing about the man in front of me.

"Not quite." I answered

"Let's eat then. I know a great place." he paused briefly, smiling all the while "Ready?"

"Yup." I replied, grinning back as I slid on my coat and stuffed my wallet and lip gloss into the pockets.

"You won't be needing that." he said matter-of-factly and pointed to my purse.

"Just in case" I grinned, excitement brewing deliciously in my stomach.

We headed down the stairs of my apartment block and out the doors, it was then I was faced with a glorious red sports car, which Amadore was now heading towards, and opening the passenger side door.

"After you, Miss Jones." he beamed as he saw me take in his car with awe "Like what you see? Jaguar F-type."

"It's.... sexy as hell." I grinned as I bit my lip and peered to see his reactions through my eyelashes.

"Like something else I know." he replied with a wink, making the butterflies in my belly almost explode into my throat. *He's not talking about you, stupid!* my conscience barked at me, hurting me. "Hop in." he added.

Settling into the extremely hot car, I buckled up and watched him do the same, shifting the seat back and checking the mirror, he dared a glance at me, I wondered if he could sense how warm I was getting, the butterflies were beginning to make me sick. Heat was radiating from my cheeks; I was hoping my skin wasn't as red at it felt. I wasn't used to this, I felt like I was hurling myself in the deep end, unsure if I was capable of any of this, yet here I was... And more importantly, I wanted to be here.

"It's not far from here, just don't want you slipping anymore." he said with a second wink, sending the butterflies into a frenzy.

"Sorry..." I muttered, feeling clumsy and stupid.

"Don't ever apologize to me, Anabelle." he breathed. I nodded, not knowing if I was capable of that either.

He handled the car like I imagined, everything else in his life, with power and edge. It brought feelings and thoughts to my mind that I thought would never appear, I was suddenly very aware how much I was attracted to him... Sexually. He held light conversation on the drive there, I told him about my boring job and he spoke some more about his, explaining how people hire him for functions and other events if they feel they need extra safety. I couldn't help but wonder if his job was dangerous, he spoke so casual about it like he could have easily been talking about being a postman or a milkman.

"It must be good money," I said tapping the dash board of the Jag.

"Very rich people will pay good money for guaranteed protection." he stated

"How is it guaranteed? Surely anything could go wrong." I asked, questioning what he said before my brain caught up and scolded me for questioning back, his smile, however, almost told me he enjoyed it.

"Of course, I've been doing it for six years though, and no one has been harmed yet - touch wood," he tapped his head as I giggled "So until they do, I'm holding my one hundred percent record."

"I see." I added as I glanced out the window. We'd arrived at our destination and it seemed we were in a small village, although I never caught the name. He unbuckled his seat belt and hopped out, heading round to the passenger side to hold my door open for me. "Thanks." I said, feeling girly.

We headed inside the sleepy pub door,

inside was warm and cozy, and smelled delicious. On the right was the bar area, where a middle aged couple sat, flirting with each other and to the left was a large dining area. It wasn't that busy, just a couple of tables taken up. One with a family of four, the other had one middle aged man eating alone. Adele sung in the back ground - begging someone to remember her, I recognized the song and smiled, it was one of my favorites. Amadore broke my reverie, asking the young waitress for a table for two - in the corner. She flushed and smiled, immediately jumping to his request. I noticed that perhaps I wasn't the only one weak to his charm.

  Settling into our cozy table in the corner, I shrugged off my coat and he took it from me, handing them both to the waitress while she giggled and flirted with him, before scurrying off to hang them up and fetch her order pad. I sunk into the comfy arm chair and instantly began fiddling with the napkin on the table, wanting to admire the view of the homely restaurant yet I couldn't seem to take my eyes off Amadore. There was a small part of me beginning to wonder if there was any view more spectacular. I was starting to wonder who I was becoming and how the hell it was happening, how was he doing the impossible to me? I ran into him, literally, yesterday night, and now - here we are. There was something else to him, I knew it. He'd drawn me in, but then again... I wasn't complaining.

"What would you like to drink?" Amadore asked as he interrupted my day dream and I noticed the waitress stood there, seemingly not too pleased, jealously smeared across her face.

"Oh... Erm... Just a Pepsi I think." I answered feeling under pressure from her gaze.

"Make that two, please." he added, never taking his eyes off me. I chanced a look at her from under my eyelashes just in time to catch her scowl at me before heading off.

"I don't think she likes me, jealously is a terrible thing." I joked as I glanced back to him, and almost losing myself in his sweet, delectable gaze.

"With your looks, you must get that a lot." he replied, still claiming my eyes.

"Oh, I didn't mean... Erm... I meant... Because of who I'm sat with." I stuttered trying to explain myself but quickly feeling foolish. At that moment he grinned a heart stopping grin, and almost seemed to blush. He looked away for a spilt second, not wanting his eyes to give him away. My breath hitched. I was mesmerized.

"Let's change the subject, I think," he returned his eyes to mine "Do you have any siblings?"

We chatted for hours that evening, about me being an only child, about his 'annoying' brothers Bernardo (the eldest at thirty years old) and Carlos (the youngest at twenty-one). Amadore was the middle child, he was twenty-five. He touched briefly on his parents, explaining that they had both passed away when he was young. Once again, reminding me never to apologize to him. I wondered who had cared for him growing up, but decided not to pry. He asked questions about my up-bringing too.

"And, your parents?" curiosity spread across his beautiful features.

"Are fine, I presume." I offered the only answer I had for him. A part of me, given a very small part, thought about sharing my horrific upbringing, but quickly dismissing the idea. Selfishly I didn't want to lose him, yet. How do you possibly explain that your father abused you for two years, then your mother resented you for breaking up her happy home, then almost being the outcast in the family. The dirty thing that destroyed it all.

He sensed that a conversation change was in order and began asking about my job and for the most part, I really had nothing great to say about that either. I saw something that looked like anger in his caramel eyes when describing my perverted boss, but he hid it well, that or he was bored and frustrated at the dull conversation I had to offer.

Three hours flew by, as we enjoyed a wonderful meal of starters, main, dessert and I was just finishing my coffee as I realized the time.

"You need to get home?" he asked as he caught me checking my watch.

"Kind of, I have work in the morning." I stated as he grinned a relaxed, perfectly heartwarming grin.

"Let's get you home then."

Obviously, he insisted on walking me to my door, the ride home had been just as relaxed and fun as the evening, just with an extra added side of lust. Watching him drive his big, red toy did something to me that had never happened before. I had never been wanted, or wanted anyone... until now.

"So, perhaps I'll call you, if that's okay? I'd like to see you again, Anabelle." he breathed as he leaned in my doorway.

"I... Erm... I don't have a phone." I stuttered, what twenty-year-old didn't have a phone, I felt so ashamed.

"You giving me the brush off, Miss Jones?" Amusement mixed with concern tickled the edges of his face.

"No, definitely not, I'd like to see you again too, but I still don't have a phone." Reassuring him, although he knew that wasn't the case.

"What time do you finish work tomorrow?" he questioned again as my hopes raised.

"Four... Nine' till four tomorrow."

"Good. Can I meet you afterwards?" he proceeded as my inside melted away. I considered playing it cool, telling him I was busy, but instead I went with "That would be nice."

"Good, four o clock then. See you there." and with that, he left.

I walked around, getting ready for bed, singing and occasionally giggling out loud. For the first time in nine years, I felt care free... happy. Entering my bedroom from my bathroom, dressed in yet another set of childish pajamas, I noticed a black crow sat on my window sill. I smiled as his head turned to the side, like he'd seen me too. I walked up to the window slowly, careful not to scare him away and knelt down, he still sat there, watching me.

"Hello, Mr. Crow" I said, aware I was talking to a bird, but then again, sometimes everyone needs someone to talk to, sadly for me... the best I've got is a bird. "Did you see him? The man that brought me home? He was lovely, wasn't he?" I paused in thought as I glanced up at the stars, they were so clear and sparkling charmingly. "I felt new tonight... like... perhaps I don't have to be this lonely, pathetic excuse anymore... like I could be someone else with him... if my head allows it. Until obviously, he finds out about my dad..." My thoughts veered off, imagining him running miles when he realizes how screwed up I am. "Night, Mr. Crow." I said as I drew the curtains and climbed into bed.

I dreamt that night about Amadore once more, he caught me again, saving me as I fell, apart from this time... after he caught me, he swooped me up and kissed me passionately. Not only did I let him... I enjoyed it.

Chapter 5

My alarm jerked me awake at seven thirty, tearing me from my dream which, as the night progressed, had got rather heated. I woke up with sweat on my forehead and a racing heart. I sat up and put my head in my hands "What are you doing to me, Mr. Renato?" I sighed as I flung my legs over the edge of the bed. Four o' clock seemed so far away, and for reasons unknown to me, I wished for it to come sooner. I went straight to the shower and slid in, welcoming the heat of the water as it washed over my skin, the beat of the spray on my face washing away memories of last night's dream that I desperately clung to. I knew what sex was, too well at times, it had always seemed... foul. What cheap, dirty prostitutes did. Parting my legs so somebody could have a good look was wrong, I was wrong... my father was wrong. But... not last night, that wasn't wrong. In fact, it couldn't have felt more right, more romantic, more tender and sweet. I hopped out of the shower and headed to the sink to brush my teeth, as I scrubbed away I stared into my eyes, they seemed lighter than usual, normally they sat at a dull grey tone, but this morning, they seemed blue. Bright blue. There were no dark circles around my eyes either just bright, awake and full of life eyes. I spat the toothpaste down the sink and smiled at myself in the mirror, a smile which - for all intents and purposes - would tell the world I was happy. Perhaps I was.

Chucking on my uniform consisting of my white shirt - one size too small, black skirt and tights and black pumps, I shoved my apron, book and wallet in my bag, grabbed a banana for the journey and set out. It was cold still so I pulled my zip up on my coat and shoved my hands in my pockets. Arriving at work with just enough time to chuck my bag in my locker, hang up my coat and tie my apron on.

"Morning, Anabelle." Steve's voice droned behind me, making me jump and turn round. He was stood in the doorway of the staff room, blocking the exit.

"Morning, Steve." I returned, feeling uneasy.

"The cook has called in sick, we're just waiting for cover to arrive before we open up, shouldn't be long though. Half hour, tops." His eyes were exploring my body and I cowered under his glare. A bead of sweat trickled down his forehead and he wiped it with his sleeve, repulsing me.

"Okay, I'll set up the restaurant while we wait." I offered, not stepping forward as he was still in the way. His gaze lingered on me for too long, I began to feel awkward and sick "Excuse me." I said, my tone strong and forward. He thought for a moment, then laughed, coughing in between and making me step backwards, watching carefully the whole time. After what seemed like an eternity he turned on his heels and wobbled off to take his seat in the office, where I was sure he'd spend most of the day. I couldn't help the shudder vibrating over my body, the sicko really creeped me out.

My work day dragged on too long, full of grumpy business men stopping by for coffee and toasted teacakes, I busied myself all day, desperate for the time to go faster. When four a clock rolled around I couldn't help the spring in my step as I headed to the staff room to grab my things. I decided not to say good bye to Steve, merely because I didn't want to risk any sort of conversation he might want to have. I just waved to Chris, the stand in cook and Shellie, the closing waitress. I headed out of the door to have my breath snatched from my lungs... There he was.

Leaning against the red Jaguar, chatting on the phone with his stunning hair occasionally blowing over his face then settling back on his shoulders. Of course his trademark duffle coat covered his, from what I imagined, impeccable body, teamed with dark jeans and smart shoes. He noticed me too and hung up on whoever he was talking to, offering me a smile which warmed my skin yet left goose bumps at the same time. I tried as carefully as I could not to slip as I headed over to him, I peeked up to see delight playing in his eyes, watching me carefully. I made it to him safely and smiled, feeling somewhat proud of myself.

"Hello, beautiful." His greeting almost sweeping me off my feet, I had to remind myself to breathe and reply.

"Hello." I whimpered back, unworthy of his words "You didn't need to pick me up from here, I could have met you at mine."

"Yes, I know, but I have something for you, hop in." He ordered as he opened the passenger door for me. I obliged and slid in welcoming the warmth from the car as he closed the door. The music on the stereo stood out, it was a song I loved called 'I'm yours'. I'd adjusted the volume to hear it better as he slid in the driver's side and looked at me.

"One of your favorites?" he asked as I bit my lip and nodded shyly, the lyrics are so raw and touching that the song has always had the power to hush me, but right now I wasn't sure if it was the song or the gorgeous man staring deep in my eyes. He broke eye contact for a brief moment as he reached into the back then handed me a box.

"Here," he said as he placed it on my lap. I looked down and in my hands sat a box containing a brand new BlackBerry "I took the liberty of setting it up for you, I didn't know how good you were with technology." His words drifted off as he examined my face. "So... can I have your number then...? Or...?"

"I... I can't accept this." I was so aware that this was far too much, far too soon, three days since I fell into his world, and he is already buying me mobile phones.

"I'd really like it if you did." he responded, still searching my face.

"I'll pay for it, how much did it cost? I'll go to the cash point now." I wanted to make him happy, and accepting the phone would but I couldn't... So compromise was the correct route.

"You don't need to do that." he answered as I made eye contact, something in his golden eyes deepened, like they were reaching into me, they were in my head. I could feel them draw me in like a fish on a hook. I felt my control and everything I believed was true slowly slip from my mind. He blinked and suddenly looked away, gripping the steering wheel briefly then starting the car. I felt like they had let me go, like I returned to myself as quickly as I had disappeared. "Please accept my gift, Anabelle. It would make me very happy." he seemed angry, but perhaps more at himself. I didn't understand why.

"Okay… Thank you, Amadore." I smiled, wanting his happiness more than my next breath. He turned to me, bliss glistening in his eyes.

"Anabelle, it was my pleasure." I wanted to laugh at how unbelievably gorgeous and persuasive he was. Instead, I sunk into the leather chair, and enjoyed the rest of the song as he drove us home, I stopped breathing as he started singing along.

"I may not have the softest touch… I may not say the words as such… I know I don't fit it that much… but I'm yours" he offered me a cheeky half grin, like he almost knew what he was doing to me, he was running my emotions ragged, untying every thread that held me together. This wasn't me and I knew it, I was incapable. It was like he had just strolled into my life and decided to make some changes and I couldn't do a damn thing about it. I could just stand on sidelines and witness him correct my life to how he believed it should be. A part of me felt anger at him, but the most part had completely no control. He had weakened every sense I own, leaving me breathless.

I was so glad when we arrived back at my flat, I unbuckled my seat belt quickly and hopped out of the car before he had a chance to open my door, I almost gasped for cold air in my lungs, to snap me out of my reverie, to ground me again.

"You OK?" he asked as he reached my side, noticing my quick exit from the car.

"What are you doing to me? Why are you doing this?" I asked before my self-control could kick in, almost shocking myself with the words flooding out of my mouth.

"I don't know what you mean," he answered, obviously confused at my childish outburst. "I like you, Anabelle. I'm just trying to get to know you."

"Well... don't. You'll get hurt." I spluttered

as fear pricked in my eyes, not fear of me this time, but fear for him. He was heavenly, and I was going to hurt him eventually. Feeling the real me take control I shoved the blackberry box in his hands and quickly rushed to my door, desperate to get distance, to give him the opportunity to run. I wanted him to, I didn't deserve him, he needed the chance to leave.

    I buzzed myself in and ran up the stairs as tears began to stain my face, fumbling with my keys I let myself into my flat and collapsed on the floor, sobbing. He would undo me completely, with ease and I couldn't let him, for his sake. There is no way a heavenly creature like him deserves a head case like me. The door buzzed... and buzzed again, and again. I pulled myself together briefly, got to my feet and held down the intercom.

    "Amadore..." I began but he interrupted,

    "Anabelle, please let me in... please." I pressed the door release and heard him begin to take the stairs instantly so I stood at the door, waiting for his face to inevitably take my breath away. And it did. It broke my heart as well because concern plagued his eyes and a crease between his brow looked painful, he walked straight up to me, close... very close, but kept his hands at his side.

"Anabelle... I want to know you... you can't hurt me, I swear." He held out his hand, willing me to take it, offering his trust for mine in return "I have... secrets too... secrets which I'm afraid of." I looked into his eyes, he was being truthful with me, honest with me. Baring himself to me as a peace offering, creating an even balance for me to stand on, something to start with. I took a breath in and held it there, placing my hand in his. His fingers wrapped around my hand, and there was no fear. Just faith. Hope. I blew my breath out of my lungs, relief creeping up from my hand and sweeping over my body. I thought of the secrets he was keeping. His dark eyes were smoldering, needing me to believe in them. There was something in them, something screaming out of them. His secrets laid there, I knew that for certain. I imagined him telling me he was secretly a God or something, I realized I would believe that, without needing any proof.

"I'm a complicated person, Amadore... bare that in mind." I warned as I squeezed his hand in return, the first contact I'd felt since I was thirteen... I felt him fill the lonely void that had cemented a spot inside of me for too long.

I never wanted him to leave.

Chapter 6

The following day had me smiling to myself from the moment I opened my eyes and the whole time I attempted to get ready for work. I couldn't really understand why Amadore felt the need to care for me, to get to know me. But he did. Although I had immense fear of him actually knowing me, knowing my secrets, I wanted him around. He was a breath of fresh air to me, blowing all the cobwebs away.

My intercom buzzed loudly just as I was about to leave off for work at eight thirty am. Confused, I headed over and picked up the receiver, aware I had to leave soon if I didn't want to be late.

"Hello?"

"Morning. Want a ride?" Amadore's sweet voice sung down the phone, sending an explosion of butterflies in the pit of my stomach and a smile so wide it hurt.

"Oh…" I stuttered, half laughing. How was he this perfect? Guys like him just don't exist "That would be great." I managed.

"That's good. I brought coffee too. You like coffee?"

"Yes, Coffee is good."

"Excellent. I'll wait here." it was so hard to listen to his words when his voice made me swoon. *Concentrate, Belle!* my conscience would scorn.

"Okay." I hung the receiver back and scrabbled to grab my stuff before heading out of the door. I didn't know whether to sprint down the stairs of my apartment block, or walk slowly. I wanted to see him, wanted to look in his eyes. I craved the sound of his voice and how it smoothed over me like honey. But I wanted to savor this moment. Deep down I knew, once he finds out how screwed up my past is, he'll bolt. But until then, I get this. I get to see his face. Hear his voice. Smell his scent. I shook my head at the crazy thoughts in my head and sucked in a deep breath, just to have Amadore steal it away the moment I opened the door.

For the next two weeks, we comfortably settled into a routine. On my days off he made plans for us to do different things together, meals out, drives to the coast to see the stars - he said it was his favorite place to count them. We even made a trip into town to watch the Christmas lights being switched on. The different colored lights sparkling on his divine face made me lost for words, so much so he had to ask me three times if I would like a mince pie. On days when I was working he would always be waiting, stood at the passenger side door of his Jag, grinning his award winning smile as I exited my workplace, whatever time it was. I had told him countless times that it wasn't necessary, but he stood firm, claiming it made him feel better knowing I was home safe. I would also ask offer him in for a mug of tea, whatever the time and he would always accept my offer, whatever the time. Just over two weeks ago, I had nobody, I was desperately lonely and although I didn't know it, I'd craved human contact so badly I'd excluded myself from everywhere, now I had two friends. One obviously being Amadore, who was quickly becoming the reason I woke up in the morning and the reason I wanted to sleep at night.

    My dreams made our relationship more serious, even if that was the only place it was right now. He hadn't made another move to touch me in any way since he held my hand, for that I was grateful. He was taking his time to earn my trust, leading me to the point of almost insanity. I craved him now but too afraid to do anything about it. He was tormenting me in all the right ways, he'd catch me often looking at him, watching him drive or wetting his lips with his glorious tongue. I'd have to bite my lip to stop myself making any rash decisions. He'd always grin at me, like he knew what he was doing, fucking tease. The second friend being the crow, inventively named 'Mr. Crow' who had decided to set up camp on my window sill. He was a large bird, one of the biggest I'd seen and he was very intrigued in me. He'd often glare in at me as I danced around my bedroom, singing to my favorite songs, imagining my other worldly stranger singing with me. I talked to him often too, about Amadore of course. It may seem strange, but when most girls get a crush they call all their friends up to tell them about it, so I'd seen in movies anyway. I didn't have that luxury, so a bird was a good second best.

    This particular day, day sixteen of my life involving Amadore, I had work, bad times. However, my shift was almost over and the rush of the customers had died down. Steve had locked the front doors for the night, leaving me and Shellie to clean tables and begin closing down, it was nine o clock and I knew, without any doubt,

Amadore would be waiting for me when I finished. When I closed the restaurant I had got into a routine of texting him ten minutes before I knew I'd be done and he would always respond with a simple "On my way, beautiful." He was always on time and equipped with a heart stopping smile, just for me. Sadly, for me, I still had a good two hours of cleaning to do but I was hurrying, working hard, excited for the moment I got to see him again.

As always, I heard Steve behind me before I even turned around, I was bent over wiping down tables and was instantly aware of his presence so quickly spun around, cutting off his view.

"I've sent Shellie home; she had finished in pot wash." He stated, his eyes searching my body, I noticed that he was making less eye contact than usual, in fact he was making none at all.

"Everything OK?" I asked, trying to seem calmer than I was, his mood and shifty eyes were really unnerving me.

"The cook has gone home too." he added as beads of sweat pricked at his forehead.

"Oh, okay." I stepped back slightly, hoping he wouldn't notice. My breath hitched in my throat as I watched his fingers twitch. Something was wrong. I could almost smell the danger I was in and I knew in that moment that I had to escape. I glanced towards the kitchen, knowing that the fire exit was my best bet. My escape route... then he dived towards me.

The first thing I felt was his hand in my hair, pulling it back hard exposing my neck. Fear struck me like once before, memories flooding my mind, open wounds exposing the depths of my panic. I'm almost positive my scream was ear piercing as I scratched, hit and slapped at his sweaty body, desperately trying to break free from his grip, but he was too strong. I heard the buttons of my shirt scattered across the floor as I was revealed to him.

"Please!!" I yelled, following it with a scream full of dread and horror. He forced me on to the table, holding me by the throat as his hands tugged at my bra. It was going to happen again, I felt my mind closing down my body becoming numb, the fight in me dying, my soul with it. I pressed my eyes closed as tears streamed down the sides of my face. It was like my whole world was crashing down around me, tearing apart any threads that I had sown together so delicately. I chanced one more slap using up the rest of my will power. It was then he flew across the restaurant, smashing into a table before landing with a crash on the floor.

Eyes wide and my heart beating fast, I stared straight into the caramel eyes of Amadore.

"It's okay." he whispered to me softly as he shrugged off his duffle coat and placed it over my shoulders, I clung to it, wrapping it around my chest to cover my bra, which was now on show displaying a broken strap. He turned on his heels and stalked over to Steve. Amadore, ever the predator, had his eyes locked on his prey, who was now bleeding from a cut on his head and rolling around on the floor trying to find his feet. Grabbing hold of his collar, Amadore hauled him to his feet with incredible strength, not even struggling with Steve's weight and gazed straight into his eyes, something shifted in the air as he spoke clearly, directly to Steve

"*Listen to me carefully, you stupid fucker. You will regret this day for the rest of your short life, months you will sink into a depression, devastated at what you have done... Then you will kill yourself.*" His voice was menacing as he threatened him, full of anger and animalistic rage.

"Amadore...?" I whimpered wanting to leave, not wanting to see anymore, needing to run... but to run with him. He was by my side quicker than humanly possible. I put it down to my delusional state, I needed to go home, shower and never return here and I needed to go now.

"Let me carry you." It wasn't a question; it was a demand... But a welcome one. I slid my arms into the sleeves of his coat and slung them around his neck, he swooped me into the safety of his strong grasp then stalked towards the locked door and kicked it open, breaking it off at its hinges. I was in the Jag in seconds and he almost flew around to the driving seat, sparking the car to life and shooting off in the direction of my flat. I sobbed hard all the way home until we parked outside my apartment block. Without thinking I reached into my apron pocket and handed him the keys. He took them without question then appeared at the passenger door, lifting me out and holding me tight. I was still sobbing into his shoulder as I heard the key turn in the lock and felt the warmth of my flat soothe my skin. I still didn't open my eyes. I had gone back to being eleven again. What I couldn't see wasn't real. What I could feel I'd block out, causing myself pain by biting on the inside of my cheek. I felt myself slipping away. It was the rush of water which brought me back, I was still curled in Amadore's arms, still sobbing profusely. I tensed and squeezed him closer towards me as the downpour got warmer. I blinked a few times and opened my eyes to meet his, to find my way back to him. We were in my shower, fully clothed and drenched right through. He just stood there, holding me, staring at me as I fought my inner battle. Drops of water slid off his stunning facial features, his dark eyelashes, the ends of his auburn hair, dripping off his nose onto my face. There it was, my landing strip, my reasoning, my sanity, it was all there in his eyes, found so easily, given to me so purely.

 He slowly placed me on my feet and the space between us seemed too much. He felt so far away. I run my hands over the back of his neck, up into his hair as a heavy breath escaped his lips. He held eye contact as he knew that's what I needed, I had known him for only two weeks but he had become the only thing I knew, what I now needed to survive. As I felt his hand touch so lightly on my waistline, my body bowed to him. I don't know when it started or where he came from but I knew he was here to save me, to always save me.

"Kiss me..." I purred as I needed more of him, needed him to fix me, needed him to change the memory of tonight, to turn it and make it good. I saw him think for a moment, staring into my eyes for answers I wasn't giving away. He lent in... paused for a brief moment before making his decision... Then he kissed me.

Chapter 7

His kiss was demanding and possessive, yet gentle and seductive. He pulled me at my hips, needing closeness as I did. Following his lead, I pulled at his hair gently, needing to possess him also, needing whatever he had to offer me. In that single moment I found everything I had been waiting for. Water rushed over us, washing away all things cruel and bad, leaving us new, revived... ready for each other.

"Wait..." he breathed, gasping for air, staying close to me, holding me still. "Where are all... your things? ... Your bag?" he stuttered, seeming as lost for words as I was, he couldn't wait for a response before claiming my lips again, kissing me deeper and more passionate, if that was possible, his tongue entered my mouth, caressing mine, his invasion was one I craved, almost depended on.

"Still at work." I mumbled in between kisses, not wanting to stop. Wanting this moment to last forever.

"Okay..." his grip tightened as his kiss deepened. I heard a growl in his throat, confirming he was perhaps enjoying this as much as I was. "I'll get it later."

"Wait…" I hummed this time, making him stop instantly and pull back, I smiled as I held on, pulling him back closer to me, his eyes lightened, grinning as he closed the distance, "Your clothes are wet." I said as a husky chuckle escaped me, thoughts of him soaking his new Jag's leather interior shouldn't have been as funny as it was.

"Right, because that's what I'm thinking about at this exact moment in time." sarcasm dripped off his voice like the water off his eyelashes as he returned my chuckle with a glorious laugh of his own. "I'm not worried about my clothes… I'm worried about you." he continued, his smile turned serious and concerned.

"I'm OK, I was lucky you were there… two hours early." I registered as I felt the crease between my brow deepen "Why were you there so early?"

"Anabelle… we need to talk." he breathed as his concern washed over me as well.

"Did I do something wrong?" I asked, terrified he was about to leave.

"No, God no!" he quickly added, placing both hands on my face and holding me still, looking into my eyes. "There is something about me you should know. I perhaps should have told you sooner. I'm just... afraid to frighten you away." he kissed my forehead to soften the blow, but I was scared, scared he was leaving, scared I got this far with him and now he is making his excuses to leave.

"Don't leave me." I whimpered, taking my arms and wrapping them round his waist, holding on close and resting my head on his chest. His heart was racing, like mine.

"I'm going to pop to the car, I have spare clothes there. Have a shower. When you come out, I'll be here... with tea... ready to talk... and maybe kiss you some more, if you'll let me." he added with a grin.

"Promise you won't leave?" I asked, seeming too desperate.

"I promise I won't leave." he assured me, kissing me once more and exiting the shower.

I stripped off his coat, followed by my clothes and chucked them with a soggy thump onto the bathroom floor before scrubbing myself clean, my neck was red raw before I'd done. Tears came from my eyes, but I refused to cry properly, I was saved... for the first time ever, I was rescued. From the man who has been saving me ever since I ran, smack- bang, into his life, and he promised he wouldn't leave.

I hopped out of the shower and wrapped a towel around me, I heard the kettle boiling in the kitchen and smiled. Heading into the bedroom, I grabbed my blue fleece pajamas out of my drawers and chucked on a white vest. I looked into the mirror before leaving, my hair was tied back in a messy knot and was leaving my neck bare, raw and red... *it'll fade*... I thought to myself as I chucked the towel into the wash basket and headed out into the kitchen/lounge area. Of course, Amadore was there, dressed in dark blue Levi jeans and a crystal white t-shirt, cut in a V-neck, showing a tiny amount of his perfect body. his hair was still wet, so he'd tied it back, he looked every bit the God I thought he was, even his bare feet seem so delectable, so irresistible.

He strolled over to me carrying two mugs of steaming hot tea and kissed my forehead.

"Sit down, Princess." he said in almost a whisper, and I did what he said, curling up on the sofa and hugging my knees to my chest. All sorts of thoughts and feelings flowing through me, I was intrigued about him, I wanted to know everything about him, all the deep and dirty ins and outs, but he was making a big deal out of this and it was beginning to put me on edge.

"What is it?" I asked, not moving closer as he sat down beside me, placing the mugs on the coffee table in front of us and scooting back in the chair, facing me.

"I am who you think I am, whatever I've said to you since knowing you... I meant every word. But at the same time... I'm not what you think I am..." His words drifted off as shock succumbed me.

"You're a woman?" I asked, voice shaken, only to be made to jump by Amadore's heavenly laugh, bellowing loudly, easing my shock "I'm glad this is amusing for you." I added with a scowl.

"Do you think I'm a woman?" he asked, still laughing as he placed his hand on my knee "Sorry," he chuckled again "No, princess- I'm definitely a man." his hand squeezed my knee, weakening my senses.

"Please don't be so quizzical." I begged, wanting this conversation to end now, I needed him to tell me what was on his mind so I could accept him, anyway he chooses to give himself to me, and we could carry on.

"I kind of have to be... I need you to think about what you've seen tonight, I need you to work it out." his eyes had turned serious again "This world isn't all you think it is." he added, forcing me to think deeper, focus more. What had I seen…?

"Your fast…" I said, my eyes drifting from his to gain composure, to think harder. My breath caught in my throat as I truly thought about what I was about to say. What I was about to suggest. I knew I had seen it with my own eyes. But it wasn't true… was it? "Really fucking fast." I stated, remembering him move at the restaurant and recalling being carried by him, doing the length of the car park in milliseconds. His head nodded and I continued "You were there at work… at the right time….. you… see the future?" I asked as he's head shook. His eyes were deadly serious, reading my soul for any sense of fear.

"Not quite… I heard you scream." he offered, helping me.

"From the car park?"

"From my house." I vaguely remembered a conversation we had on the beach, under the stars.

"You live… out of town." I stuttered, unsure to believe what I was hearing, struggling to understand what I was saying. "You've got good hearing... really fucking good hearing."

"You frightened?" he asked as I met his gaze, how could I be? He saved me, if he was going to hurt me, he would have left me there.

"I'm a little confused." I answered honestly, needing proof "Show me." I added as I stood, offering him a weak glance which meant *stay there*. He didn't move, just watched me contently as I walked into the bedroom and closed the door. Walking into the furthest corner I stood facing the wall and took a deep breath "My middle name... is Diana" I whispered as quietly as I could. Positive that there was no way he could have heard, I turned and entered the lounge again and looked into his eyes.

"How fitting..." he swooned and grinned at me.

"What is?"

"It means *Heavenly, divine*." I swallowed a nervous lump that had got caught in my throat. He couldn't have heard...

"what does...?"

"Diana..." *holy shit*... I nervously walked over to the couch and sat back down. My mind continuously assuring me that it was no big deal, *breathe, Anabelle*...

"What else?" I asked, needing the whole story, knowing that he had more to give, he swallowed hard and closed his eyes. Taking a deep breath, he opened them and offered a look of sympathy towards me.

"You want more?" he asked, fear and determination prickling over his gorgeous features, his eyes seemed darker than normal.

"I want all of you, Amadore." I breathed as I placed my hand over his, which was again resting on my knee.

"Be sure you do, Anabelle." he warned as he leaned in and took my view, claiming it. I couldn't look away, I tried with everything in me. "Hear what I'm saying, hear every word... more importantly, hear your response." he ordered as he took his hand and brushed my cheek lightly, caressing me, calming me "Are you thirsty?" he asked, out of the blue.

"... No." I answered honestly, going along with him, trusting him.

"*Yes, you are...*" and I was, incredibly, beyond any doubt. My hand reached for my throat as I breathed in, the air feeling like hot razor blades slicing my throat. I went to stand, needing water more than oxygen, and needing it now.

"Wait," he grabbed my arms and took me in, I couldn't move again, I could just stare deep into his eyes "You said no, remember?" he reminded me as the thirst dulled. I did. I said no, I wasn't thirsty... I wasn't. was I? No. It dulled and drifted as I felt my body return to me, becoming mine.

"What... What the hell was that?" I stuttered as my hand fell from my throat, shock and confusion owning my face, I stood up needing space, this time he let me.

"Mind control." he murmured, looking down, looking ashamed.

"How many times have you done that to me?" I asked, anger rising like bile in my throat, he didn't reply "How many times, Amadore?!" I asked again, fury gripping me. "Tell me what I'm feeling for you are my feelings, not ones you created." my words appeared to smack him hard, his eyes darted up to meet mine, scolded by what I'd just said.

"I had to use it on you the night we met, I had to. You were frightened, and the next day at the store as it still played on you. But I have not used it on you in two weeks. I swear it. Believe me, please. Your feelings for me, whatever they are, are yours." he rose off the seat to meet me, taking both my hands. I quickly took a step back, needing to think straight, knowing his skin on mine would make me weak.

"Why was I frightened...?" I couldn't remember, I had vague memories of a man, in a long coat, but that was nothing, wasn't it?

"You were followed... he was... like me." he didn't want to open up, didn't want to tell me, but he had no right. It was my life, my fucking memories, who the hell was he to invade my mind and take whatever he chose to.

"It wasn't nothing, was it?" Knowing my thoughts weren't true, it was bad and I was in danger, it became so clear.

"He followed you, he knew where you lived. I made you leave your window open... so I could protect you."

"You broke into my home?!" I spat, my brain fighting desperately to work out what the hell was going on.

"No, he did! I was just there to remove him." his eyes looked down at me, golden and glorious while his brows knitted together tight, hurt by my outbursts.

"Why did he want to kill me?" my voice turned into almost a whisper,

"I don't know why... but I wasn't going to let that happen. I had already fallen for you." he walked closer to me, still needing closeness.

"Steve...." I choked, remembering what Amadore had said to him "You made Steve... he'll kill himself." My hands instinctively went to my face as I felt my color drain away.

"I was angry, Ana, furious in fact," his hands went to my face as well, as he bent to get to my level, still craving the intimacy we had just thirty minutes ago in the shower "He deserves it."

"What else?" I said, unsure as to whether I agreed or not, how many other girls will Steve hurt? How many had he hurt already? Were any of them as lucky as me? There was too much to think about, too much to process. Had Amadore been there before I even knew he was there? Fighting for me as I laid in bed, dreaming of him?

"That's enough for tonight." he said, kissing my forehead then bringing me close to embrace me, his arms wrapped around my shoulders "Don't leave me, Anabelle." he pleaded, repeating what I had said.

"Don't ever use your gift on me again, unless I ask you too." I thought for a moment. The gift he has could cure me... could make me forget the two horrific years of my life. Could he erase them from my memory...? Make them vanish from my existence. Leave me whole....? Make me normal...?

I let my body sink into his, wrapping my arms around his waist, feeling the strong ripples of his toned body. I accepted him, sinking deeper into his embrace and pushing my thoughts away. "I think I need to sleep now." I sighed, feeling exhaustion demand me.

"Okay..." his voice gave him away, he was frightened he'd gone too far with me, frightened he'd scared me away. I was scared he could, in theory, get me to do whatever he wanted. Then again he could (if he wanted) tell me to forget everything he had just said, and I would. But he isn't, he was leaving me with it, trusting me with his secret. He was my guardian; he always had been. Now I realized my guardian had super powers... not really a bad thing if you ask me.

"Are you super strong?" I asked, a smile giving away all the thoughts flowing through my head, he peered down at me, unable not to send me one of his glorious smiles.

"Erm... I suppose you could say that." he grinned as he looked away, his eyes thoughtful, so beautiful. I remembered him lifting up Steve like he was a child. He was super-strong... and now - I was somewhat turned on.

"See you tomorrow?" I asked, suddenly needing composure, I had accepted him too easily, I had to think, I knew I did.

"I would like that." he assured me, kissing my forehead and heading to the door to slide on his white sneakers "What time?" he asked

"Whenever you get up." I said, already feeling the distance between us, suddenly wanting him to stay near me.

"About that...." he stuttered, seeming like a battle was raging briefly in his head "I... Erm... I don't sleep." the battle to tell me the truth had won, and left me unable to really process what he had told me.

"Like... at all?"

"Not normally. Once a week maybe... my brain needs about six hours a week... sometimes less." He nodded his head as his words spilled out awkwardly. I could tell that the most part of his brain was screaming at him to stop telling me weird things. Yet he continued. I needed his honesty. In fact, the more he spoke to me about his secrets, the more I thought I could perhaps tell him about my past... one day... maybe.

"Right." I thought for a moment "What do you do at night?" I asked, trying to seem calmer about this.

"The last two weeks have consisted mostly of thinking about you." he breathed. He was impossibly gorgeous in that moment, his need for me making him mouthwatering. He was just across the room but my body ached for his, the fact that my eyes could see him, but my hands weren't touching him left me with a throbbing which I couldn't ignore.

"Don't go." I blurted out, knowing I would fall apart if he left "Wait for me here... in my bed." My heart was thumping through my chest and I was sure his impeccable hearing could hear it like a drum bashing away next to him. He didn't appear to think twice, he knew I had accepted everything he had said, and I knew that him leaving was the last thing neither he or I wanted. He kicked off his sneakers and appeared in front of me, doing the length of the room in milliseconds, so fast that when he appeared in front of me, the gust of wind he brought with him blew stray stands of my hair back. I breathed in, shocked and somewhat impressed, a half grin and dark eyes stared down at me, his fingers curling up into my hair. My skin prickled and burned for him, for his hands on me. My insides fluttered as his eyes examined me, I couldn't stop myself from biting my lip, feeling new emotions spark to life.

"Those eyes of yours... I would trade all my powers to just read your mind." he teased, as I bit my lip again, hopelessly displaying my lust for him.

"Just because I now know you're MEGA weird, doesn't mean you can whiz round like that all the time, at least pretend to be normal." I teased back, making him burst out in a glorious laugh, one of which made me join him.

"You think I'm weird?" he laughed again

"You think you're not?" I shook my head, this was going to be one hell of a ride, one I knew, beyond any doubt, I would be enjoying 'till the very end.

Chapter 8

Light shone through the curtains as I moaned and rolled over and I smelt the gorgeous citrus scent of body wash and men's cologne before I felt his heat. I rolled into his arms and breathed him in, his chuckle bringing me closer to wakefulness. My hand found its way to his belt, peeling its way under his vest and slowly making its way up, tickling its way over the toned ripples of his perfection. He sucked in a breath, running his hand up my arm until it reached my neck. I felt him edge closer, kissing my forehead.

"Good morning." he breathed into my hair, heating me to the core, I don't know if it was that time of day, but in that moment, I wanted him... in every way. I wanted him to claim me as his own. "Sleep well?" he asked, as I stretched out briefly, then snuggled back to his side, so safe and warm.

"I did, yes." I answered, peering up at him. He was a sight too sore for eyes at this time of the morning, so gloriously radiant, ridiculously flawless. His hair fell over his face, framing his features, the auburn with gold streaks glistened and shined like the sun. His eyes, all chocolate and caramel and delicious claimed my sight, welcoming me into a new day. A light dusting of stubble framed his chin, making him seem more human than perhaps he was. I dreamt of him last night. I was falling again... he'd heard me scream and caught me really fast, really strong, smiling as he drew me into him, whispering words of acceptance as we kissed, and touched... and made love, all night. It was no wonder I woke wanting more.

"Tea?" he asked as I felt my body heat up under his glare, I didn't want tea, I wanted nothing but him. I lifted my head and pulled him closer, placing his lips on my neck.

"Kiss me here," I breathed, feeling my body take over, reaching out to claim its prize. He complied, obviously, starting light and subtle, kissing up to my ears and nibbling my ear lobes, making me groan with anticipation, then moving back down over my neck and round the collar of my vest, I felt his hand at my waist, gripping slightly before starting its journey north, under my vest. My body bowed to him, he could take anything he wanted, I would allow it. His hand stopped just beneath my breast, as he rose up to meet my gaze, a grin so stunning I had to look away and smile.

"I'm going to go put the kettle on... before I

lose control." he said as he slid his hand out from under my vest. Kissing me on the forehead tenderly, he then hopped out of bed, leaving me swelling and aching for more.

"Lose control, I don't mind!" I shot back as he turned to meet my gaze, seeming as hot and heavy as I was.

"If I start that with you, Miss Jones, I'm afraid I'll never stop." he offered as he exited the room, leaving me to sag back on the bed, pull the duvet over my face and allow my thoughts to drift back to my dream.

I purposely took my time showering and making myself presentable, making him wait and getting a kick out of it too. Searching for a figure hugging outfit, I decided on my (very tight) light blue skinny jeans, a nude long sleeved, and low cut - top and my Ugg boots. I'd blow dried my hair, and tied it up in a long dark pony tail, leaving curls cascading down my back. I was ready to tease Mr. Renato, and job hunt - of course.

"Took your time, Miss Jones." Amadore stated, seated on a stool by the breakfast bar, waiting patiently. His eyes looked me up and down, a half grin creeping up on his face like he knew my game, he knew exactly what I was doing. I turned and walked away from him over to the lounge and felt his eyes burn into me, trying to work me out. With my back towards him, I bent over. Picking up my phone which was on charge. Standing up he was right where I wanted him, pressed against my back, breathing down my neck. "What's the matter, princess?" he whispered in my ear, sparking up my senses like a revving car.

"Nothing..." I offered, turning on the spot to face him, pressing my body against his. I was a different girl today, I knew it. I felt no longer plagued by memories, I was driven by my future, my desire to spend every second with this man, my superman.

"You look lovely... Going somewhere nice?" he asked, amusement playing behind his eyes.

"Job hunting, then hopefully spending the evening with you." I replied, my eyes searching his for his answer.

"You don't need to go job hunting today, take a day off." he answered, his face disguising concern.

"Can't, I have bills to pay." I shot back.

"I'll pay them." he returned, not budging.

There was no way I would ever allow that, even if I was desperate, which I wasn't. Ever since I moved in three years ago, my mother, Katherine, has been throwing her money at me, opening me an account and putting enough in to cover rent, bills, shopping and luxuries each month. Of course I got a job and supported myself, but I had the card, just in case, probably with hundreds of thousands in.

"I have savings; I don't need your money." I said, running my hands up into his hair to soften the rejection, his hands wrapped around my waist, his eyes giving him away, he was scheming. Slowly his hands moved downwards, gently resting on my rear, a devilish half grin scorching his features. My breath hitched. I knew whatever he had just decided, he was getting his way.

"Okay, then job hunting can wait until Monday, let's enjoy the weekend together first." He planted his idea whilst slowly kissing up my neck and licking my ear lobe.

"...Okay." I groaned, arching my back and pushing my rear into his hands, his breathing sped as he gently squeezed and pulled me closer, pressing me against his toned body.

"What are you doing to me, Anabelle...?"

his voice was husky and pained as he repeated my words I had used once. He placed his lips over mine, claiming them as his own, working them until they swelled and throbbed for him, pulling away slowly, leaving me desperate for more. His hands rose back to my waist, his self-control fighting its way through.

"What do you have planned then, Mr. Renato?" I asked, knowing what I wanted his answer to be, judging by his brooding eyes, it crossed his mind too. He thought for a minute.

"Perhaps we could go to my house? I'll cook up some food." he suggested, his eyes lightening as I smiled, the idea sounding perfect.

"I'd love that." I answered with a grin "Perhaps we can talk some more about you?" I continued, knowing full well I only had half his story.

"And about you?" he asked, seemingly unsure about the ground he was about to tread, he was right to be unsure.

"No." I replied without thinking, icy feelings cooling my skin.

"Oh..." he thought for a moment "Why not?" he pressed on.

"Because..." I thought, he'd let me into his

whole world, but his deep and dark secret honestly only added to his sex appeal. My story would kill mine... and he would leave, it was simple "I don't want to lose you. Please."

"You'll never lose me, Anabelle. I want to know all of you, every part. I can't take this relationship further... until"

"Until what?" I cut him off "You mean you won't screw me until I dish the dirt?" I lashed, hurt spraying across his face, I felt bad instantly.

"That's not what I meant, I need to know you trust me. I don't want to ruin this." he pleaded.

"What do you know?" I asked, any other guy would have bedded me already, why was he worried about trust, he knew more than he was letting on, he just wanted me to say it out loud.

"Anabelle, please." he begged as I pulled away, needing distance to think clearly.

"What do you know?!" I yelled, craving answers.

"Just what you've told me... even though... you don't know you've told me." his answers were cryptic again, irritating me.

"Like, in my sleep?" I asked as he shook his head "THEN WHEN?" my patience all but gone, anger making me shake.

"You said... I'll leave when I find out about your father," his words cut me, knocked me backwards and drained me of life, he knew. "Who is he? What did he do?" he pressed on, unaware I was shutting down. He would leave once I said the words out loud. But perhaps I've been stupid. Foolish to think I could base us on lies and secrets...

"He raped me... for two years. I told my mother... but she didn't believe me. She thought I was trying to break up her happy home." tears run like rain water down my face, I was white as fresh snow and felt as cold as it too. "You can go now..." I finished, the fight had beaten me.

Amadore was stood, frozen in front of me. I could just about see his hands, shaking violently. He was breathing heavy as my eyes met his, fury raged behind them.

"I..." he stuttered, searching for words "I didn't realize... I thought that..." I interrupted him by collapsing, tears burst through my barriers, I wasn't ready to go back to my lonely life. I had Amadore now. I couldn't lose him. He caught me, of course, seconds before I hit the floor. "No, baby. Stop crying," he pleaded as he grabbed my shoulders, shaking me, forcing me back to him

"Should I make you forget?" he asked, desperation pulsing through him "Please baby, I'm not leaving, I swear it, stop crying." he pulled me towards him, embracing me, kissing my hair. "You want to know how I knew?" he asked as I looked up to him. But I had already realized. His hearing. I chat away to myself all the time. Myself or that fucking bird. He heard me.

"Your hearing. You heard me." I said, knowing I was right, kicking myself for not realizing before.

"Not quite…" he said as he rose to his feet. "You trust me?" he asked, as I glared up at him.

"Yes…" I whimpered.

"You promise not to leave me?" he questioned.

"Promise." I sniffled, feeling intrigued by his sudden conversation change.

"Good, because I trust you." was the last thing he said, before a rush of air took my breath away, blowing me backwards off my knees so I landed on my ass, I got my breath back just in time to see Amadore's clothes scattered on the floor, and a crow sat on top of them, looking straight at me.

Chapter 9

I scrambled backwards until my back hit the wall, reminding myself to breathe. The crow... Amadore, hopped forward, closer to me.

"How... How is this possible...?" I whispered, things like this just didn't exist, they were the stuff of stories, tales people told hundreds of years ago, they weren't real. They couldn't be. Shape shifting just wasn't true. I recalled every night that the crow sat on my window sill, guarding my room, it was him, him all along. But not last night...he was in my bed last night, protecting me closer, more intimately.

I cursed myself for not realizing it all along. The black crow was bigger than any I'd ever seen before and its dark inky feathers glistened in the glow of the lamp. It was by far; the most impressive bird I had ever seen... because it wasn't a bird. I needed his answers. I needed him to look at me, promise me that it would all be OK. "Amadore... come back to me." I whimpered, needing him to hold me now. I was stripped bare, as was he also. I could live with this, I could live with anything, as long as it included him. He blinded me, stealing me of all my reasoning. My secrets, my life, seemed irrelevant to his, my stories only held my self-doubt, his held his safety, his way of life. He trusted me unconditionally, as I did him,

Wind gusted into my face once more, stealing my breath. I forced my eyes to stay open, to watch him come back to me, feathers disappearing and disintegrating with sparks as the figure grew taller, transforming back to the man I had grown to adore. Grown to worship. He was a God in his own right. Within seconds he was back, stood gloriously naked in front of me. Every muscle on show and his skin sun kissed and so luscious, too faultless to walk this earth. He didn't try to cover himself up, instead choosing to just stand there, giving all of himself to me. I sat, unworthy, on the floor peering up at him, in awe of him. His face seemed distressed, unsure of whether I was accepting him. He wanted me to do or say something, but his absolute flawlessness had struck me down.

"Do you want me to leave...?" his voice gave him away, fear of dismissal and rejection inked into his eyes.

"No... I want you to come here... and kiss me." my heart was already pounding, blood pumping into my ears so loud I could hardly hear myself talk. He was in front of me in a blink and I lunged forward to meet him, claiming his lips and shoving my hands into his hair. His arms wrapped around me, one hand holding my head, possessively, the other squeezing my rear, pulling my waist close to his. I reached and pulled off my top, needed skin on skin contact I felt utterly starved of. He groaned in delight as he spun me round, laying me on the rug on the floor and pressing his body on top of mine, his lips never leaving me, making mine hot and swollen. His tongue teased mine, dipping into my mouth, urgently closing any gap between us, satisfying me with himself. I unclipped my bra briskly from the catch at the front, my bare breasts were instantly pressing to his chest as I shrugged out of the straps and chucked it across the room, he moaned into my mouth with sheer delight and took the left breast into his hand, arching my back in utter yearning, I let him explore me, kissing and sucking at my neck, working downwards until his kiss met my nipples, he could have finished me there, if he desired, but he worked his way back up, his lips searching for mine.

"I don't know if I can stop myself, Anabelle." Amadore breathed fervently into my mouth before claiming me again.

"Then don't." I pleaded, taking his naked behind in my hands and urging him on, pressing his hard length between my legs, wishing I was more naked on my bottom half than I was "I'm yours." I moaned, willing him to take me.

"Later, princess..." he breathed, saying words he knew he should, but unable to stop himself "Later...when you know more." he took both my naked breasts in his hands, his lips following, sucking and tugging, undoing me.

"There's more?" I questioned, yet I didn't care. I only cared for him, and what he was doing to me in this moment, pulling me apart and putting me back together, all the pieces sliding into the right places. His kisses headed back to my lips once more, the last one holding promises of an intense night later, then he pulled away, staring at me.

"Do I have to make you want to stop...? I can make you have to pee so badly you'll run to the bathroom, you know." he joked, happiness and delight pleased his beautiful features, so contented I couldn't stop myself from smiling.

"Really? You say that as you lie stark-bollock naked on top of me?" I shot back, making his laugh bellow in the room "What the hell makes you think I'm even capable of walking right now? Let alone running?" I continued as his laugh got louder, full of exhilaration.

"OK, OK - good point." he chuckled, kissing my nose lightly "I'll get dressed" I waited for him to roll off me, ready for the shock my body will endure when it isn't touching his, yet he stayed, his eyes looking aimlessly around the room.

"We going to just stay like this?" I asked, unsure what to say.

"Oh... I Erm... need a minute." a half grin teasing his face "You could help me out a bit by covering yourself up, ya know." he joked as I realized what we were waiting for.

"Oh..." I said, propping my weight up on my elbows, my breasts closer to him, teasing him.

"Jesus Christ, Anabelle." he groaned with pleasure, and with that I was lying alone. A chuckle escaped my lips as I looked down, half naked and desperate to be ravished. *Oh, Anabelle. Pull yourself together* my subconscious scorned as I jumped to my feet, taking my top with me to cover myself up. Amadore was stood watching me, doing up the fly on his jeans, watching me with his animalistic intent.

"As I said - there's more?" I questioned, licking my lips at the erotic sight in front of me.

"Yes... my brothers." he replied, closing the gap between us, sex screaming out from me, for him to have it with me, now.

"Oh, I see. So turning into a bird won't scare me off, but you think your brothers will?" the question seemed preposterous.

"Pretty much, yeah." he grinned "Wait and see." he growled, appearing in front of me and wrapping his arms around me "And for God sake - put some clothes on, you're driving me wild."

***

We headed out a little later than expected, mostly due to the fact it took me a little too long to put my top back on. I was too busy enjoying the raw attention I was getting from Amadore as he followed me into the bedroom. I fluttered around, swinging my top in my hand, we then spent around an hour getting heated whilst he continually reminded me to get dressed, but never giving me a chance. So it was almost four o clock when we pulled up outside what could only be described as his mansion, fit for a king.

The driveway was longer than the road I lived on, tall trees either side created an archway as we drove in between, it felt like I was entering a fairytale full of dreams and mystical creatures. Then again, I suppose I was. Excitement brewed inside me, making me sit up in my seat, peering out the window in awe. Pulling up in front of his home took my breath away. It was huge, at least 3 stories of pristine brickwork, decorated with ivy crawling up the left side, I could vaguely see a garden behind, and when I say garden, I meant a huge fucking field. And when I say huge, I mean HUGE. Light shone through the big arched windows. Even the door spoke volumes about the house, dark oak and unnecessarily big with a statement gold door knocker, reminding me briefly of number ten, Downing Street. Royalty lived here, if the Mercedes and Audi that sat outside was anything to go by. Amadore pulled the Jag up next to the other stunning cars and was quickly opening my door before I even had a chance to unbuckle my seat belt. He held out his hand to help me out.

"Nervous?" he asked, watching me closely.

"No, you?"

"Yes..." he answered honestly.

"Why? Afraid I'll embarrass you?" I questioned, afraid of the answer.

"I'm afraid my brothers will." he whispered close to me, stroking his fingers over my face, smiling contently "Remember... you promised you wouldn't leave me." he reminded me as I chuckled.

"Do they... I mean... Are they like you?" I asked, preparing myself.

"Yes and no. yes, we share the same powers, but personality wise - definitely not." he took my hand and began to lead me inside just as a tall, extremely muscular man appeared at the door. He was ripped, veins tracing down his arm, hard muscles where I didn't even know you could have muscle. He was dressed in grey jogger bottoms and a dark vest, showcasing just how huge he was. He had a towel around his neck and sweat patches on his clothes, obviously straight out of the gym. I felt Amadore's hand tighten on mine.

"Bernardo." he greeted his brother so formally it was weird. I could vaguely see how they could be brothers. His hair color was the same, and his eyes were golden and glorious like Amadore, but he was much more rough around the edges, and radiated anger and rage.

"She knows?" he growled in a low, raspy voice. I gripped Amadore's hand back, instantly feeling frightened and feeble. Unwelcome.

"She worked it out." he shot back, anger dripping from his voice.

"Bullshit." he snarled, his eyes locking on to mine. I noticed the cutest little black Labrador puppy come bounding out of the door, the idea of this giant beast of a man owning the cutest little puppy had me desperately trying not to smile as the puppy ran straight up to me and I bent down to stroke him. Amadore gripped my hand and I shot him a look, just to have my superman shake his head.

"Don't stroke the mutt." he said bitterly, shocking me at his coldness. I was learning more about Amadore, he hates pets.

"Don't be cruel." I shot back as Amadore pulled me behind him, away from the puppy. "Amadore, what's wrong?"

"Carlos, fuck off!" he yelled, sounding infuriated as a gust of wind made me grip to his duffle coat and instinctively duck behind him. "Carlos! for fuck sake!" he swore again as I peeked over his shoulder, faced instantly with

Amadore's naked brother. I hid my head again, feeling safe behind him. "Go put some clothes on, she came here to see my home, not to have a laugh at the size of your cock!" he sneered, wrapping his arm behind him and placing it on my waist, reassuring me of my safety.

"Oh, please. You're just nervous because she'll see this and want it." I couldn't see any hand gestures from my hiding place but judging from Amadore's sarcastic laugh I could only assume Carlos was pointing to his penis. I grimaced at how bad this was going.

"I really won't," I whispered under my breath, to quickly be reminded of their acute hearing, Amadore bust out in a joyous chuckle, patting my backside as Carlos stomped off. I dared to peek again, just seeing Carlos's bare arse entering the house, Bernardo still stood in the doorway.

"Come, I'll show you around." my superman swooned, pulling me out from behind.

"No, you won't." Bernardo growled back, guarding the door.

"Don't do this." Amadore shot back, standing his ground.

"Do you have any idea the danger you'll

put her in? as well as us? Associating with a human? You're fucked up, Amadore."

"This isn't your concern, I'm not asking anything of you, just acceptance and a chance for you to see what I can." he seemed calmer, trying to diffuse the situation, but Bernardo just seemed to be growing more and more frustrated.

"Tell her to forget and send her on her way." he ordered, making me ease back behind Amadore, keeping my eyes down, in case he tried mind control "Or should I make her?" he threatened as I closed my eyes tight.

"Don't you dare." Amadore snarled, losing his temper quickly.

"Or what, feathers?" Bernardo snapped, the growl in his voice was menacing, ready to tear me apart.

"Can we talk about this some other time?" Amadore was gaining his composure again, but slowly edging toward his brother as dread sunk inside me, making me feeling nauseous. I wasn't worth all this; I wasn't worth him arguing with his brothers. I was trying desperately to think of a way to stop them arguing, whispering quietly under their voices, words only they could hear. It was then another bust of wind swept over me, knocking me to the floor and stealing my breath, I shuffled backwards, terrified of the sight ahead of me, a giant black wolf circling Amadore.

I was hurt, really hurt. Unwelcome and a burden. The fight Amadore was putting up for me I was unworthy of, he could easily live quite happily without me and the drama I was quite obviously causing. Hated instantly by his family hit me hard. I was kidding myself thinking I was going to find home here, Amadore is asking for acceptance, something I'll never get.

"I want to go now." I whispered quietly, knowing he would hear.

"Now look what you've done?! Fuck off, just fuck off!" he spat at his brother as he turned and quickly appeared beside me, turning his back on Bernardo - the wolf. Tears were pricking behind my eyes and I tried fighting them, Amadore caught the first tear that dropped from my eye, grasping my face tenderly "I'm sorry, I don't know why I thought this would be a good idea, I just thought... I thought... Baby, don't cry." he pleaded with me.

It was too late; I was wounded by Bernardo's utter disregard for me. I didn't know him, and right now, I didn't want to. But was he right? Was I a danger to Amadore? I needed space, I needed to breathe. I needed to get away. I'd been accepting him blindly, never thinking for a second that I was in well over my head. I brushed my fingers lightly over his face before I rose to my feet and brushed down my behind, attempting to hold on to the shreds of dignity I had left, holding my head up was something I had learnt to be good at.

"I'm going home." I whispered, stopping my voice form cracking, unable to break down under the glare of the wolf.

"I'll drive you." he offered, I could tell he was scared, frightened he'd opened up so much, and now I would leave. Perhaps he shouldn't have, it would have been more simple and easy for him if he didn't.

"I wish to walk; I'll get a bus back to the city. Please don't follow me, Amadore." I turned on my heels and strode away, sobbing silently. I wanted him, I wanted him so bad. I didn't want to walk away, every footstep hurt me more. But feeling that disgraceful brought back hurtful memories. I needed to think, by myself. Amadore didn't follow me, instead I cried all the way home, alone.

Chapter 10

I got off the bus early, choosing to walk rather than being glared at by the other passengers. I couldn't control my tears as they flowed freely, staining my face. How did this day start so perfectly, yet end so screwed up? Trying to make sense and digest all I had learnt about Amadore hurt my head, it made me feel I was going crazy believing it all. Yet I'd seen it, seen it all with my very own eyes. Perhaps he just told me knowing I have no friends, therefore I couldn't spill his secret. My thoughts ran around and round in my head, making me feel sick and dizzy. My feet felt as heavy as cement blocks as I dragged them along, willing them to work with me. I just wanted to rewind, to go back in time, to convince him not to go to his house... to stay hidden in my bed all weekend instead.

    I passed two bars on the way home and stopped outside, I very rarely drank, yet, it seemed appropriate now to get absolutely obliterated on a whiskey or ten. I don't know why I kept walking... I just did.

    I just wanted to fly away... like Amadore. To spread my wings and swoop and soar... yet I'm just a shadow on the ground, further away from heaven... further away from him. My tears came harder as I thought about how unequal we are... and always will be. Why would God grant me this wish? Why would he send him to me...? Yet make us this way? Make my armor so thin?

  I walked slowly, stopping occasionally to glance into the sky, it was getting dark as it was almost six o' clock and the ground was turning frosty. I didn't know if I wanted to see the gorgeous black crow hovering over me or not, but I cried more when he wasn't there. I thought about calling out for Amadore, knowing he would come if I did, but Bernardo's warning still rang loud in my head, the danger Amadore would be in if anyone found out about me. I couldn't risk him, I had to let him go. My whole life I've felt like a burden; loneliness was better than that. Hurt less.

  It was six thirty when I finally unlocked the door to my flat, the warmth a long-awaited relief, I closed the door behind me and sunk to the floor, staring at the mat where we laid a little under six hours ago. I was so completed then, now- I was purposeless and felt abandoned.

  Snap out of it! my conscience chastised, willing me to function. I pulled myself up and headed to the shower, undressing on the way. Sliding in and turning on the water, letting the heat of the spray scold my skin, needing its release. It seemed like hours passed as I stood with my face to the shower head, letting the water carry away the tears. I came over so tired. Needing to forget about my romantic weekend I was supposed to have, instead settling on spending tomorrow in bed. I hauled myself out of the shower and dried myself briefly before climbing into bed naked and drifting off to a restless sleep.

Amadore was making love to me passionately, whispering how magnificent I was in my ear, begging me not to leave him. I clung to his body as our sweat caused us to stick and slide together, hopelessly glued to one another.
"You promised me... promised you wouldn't leave." he whispered in my ear, breaking my heart and making me embrace him firmer... assuring him.

I think it was my sobs that woke me, bringing me back to my dark, cold and lonely room... no Amadore. I glanced at my clock, three thirty am. Tears still trickling down my face, I was still naked and felt the need to selfishly call out for him. He was all my senses and I felt like I couldn't see or hear... perhaps even breathe without him. I have no idea when this happened... how I came to feel this way. But I did. I battled within myself, weighing up the pros and cons of getting Amadore in my bed with me. The only con being his safety.

"Amadore..." I whispered, feeling self-centered and ashamed, instantly praying he didn't hear, cursing myself for being so drawn to him. A tap on my window jerked me up, clinging the sheets to my chest to hide my nakedness. Obviously, there he sat, my Mr. Crow. Tapping on my window. I put my head in my hands and cried. *you stupid, selfish little girl* my conscience howled, sounding too much like my mother. He tapped his beak on the glass again, forcing me to look at him. Wrapping the sheets around me I stood up and opened the window as he swiftly flew in and perched on my bed. I followed and sat down beside him, daring to stroke his head.

"Stay like that for a minute..." I asked, knowing as soon as he turns into my superman, I'll become weak. But I needed to say something first. "Amadore, I don't know what danger I'll get you in, but the idea of you being in any danger is terrifying for me, I can't do that. I can't be that person, you're too precious to me. You have no idea how strongly I feel for you. I need you to always be safe and happy, otherwise I won't be able to breathe. My time with you has been the happiest I've ever been, what my father did to me left scars I never thought would heal... but your touch... cured me." I stuttered as I welled up again, feeling pathetically girly and useless. Weak and vulnerable. The powerful gust of wind blew my hair across my face and I quickly looked away, sure that when I turned round, I would be immobilized by my naked God.

"Get into bed, princess." he whispered as I kept staring away, crawling into bed and sinking into the pillows. I felt the bed dip as he slid in behind me, wrapping his muscular arm around me and began kissing my neck.

"No, Amadore, I'm trouble. You're not safe." I began as he silenced me by placing a finger over my mouth, I rolled over to face him, suddenly aware how utterly naked we both were.

"I thought it was the rudeness of my brothers which made you leave...?" His words hung in the air. The idea of him left stood at his home, watching me leave, thinking it was his doing hurt.

"No, Bernardo said you'd be in danger..."

"Do you really think I'm frightened of anyone? With you, princess, I rule this world. I don't need anyone else. This is where I'm meant to be... plus, you promised you wouldn't leave, and I'm holding you to that." his fingers slid into my hair as his thumb caressed my cheek "On a good note, that is all of me... so you can take it or leave it... leaving it isn't an option though." he grinned his half grin at me as his hair fell perfectly, framing his stunning features. He knew what buttons to press, how to make me smile and laugh, he drew it out of me like steam from a kettle. I felt a grin waver over my face, he had won this time...or in fact, I had won. Selfish me.

"I want to take it, steal it all from you... but that's selfish of me." I was cut off by his kiss, tender at first, but building into a passionately charged one, undoing me. He kissed towards my ear and quietly whispered to me.

"The life you have had, princess, you're allowed to be a bit selfish, trust me when I say we are in no danger... I'd never let anyone hurt you again." he nibbled at my ear lobe as I fought my body but it was too late, I bowed to him, never wanting him to leave, and it was true. He is my superman... no one faster, no one stronger. "Relax... and indulge yourself." those words were my release as I gave myself up to him, wrapping by arms around his neck and pulling him in, kissing him like I was never going to let go. He rolled on top taking the lead, stopping briefly to peek down the covers at my body beneath his, legs wrapped around him.

"How wonderfully naked you are, Miss Jones," he grinned as I blushed under his blistering stare "What am I going to do about that?" he asked, yet already knew. My body needed his, I was the moth to his flame, and his flame was scorching hot! I couldn't control my thoughts as his kiss burnt at my neck and hands roamed my body, words of pleasure and longing spilled from my mouth in uncontrollable outbursts. He laid on top, parting my legs with his, kissing and biting my neck as his hands stroked over my breasts, "So beautiful," he moaned as his hands journeyed downwards and rested between my legs. He stilled for a moment as he stared into my eyes, reading me, frightened to take me too far. I held his gaze and bit my bottom lip, feeling an uncontrollable smirk sweep over my face at the sight of my superman, naked and pleasing me. He was too Goddamned sexy- I knew he would finish me so quickly, his fingers began to massage my sex, so skilled and gentle. I felt something building inside me, pleasure bubbling over the surfaces of my soul.

"Make love to me..." I purred, needing all of him, every part.

"I've come a little unprepared, princess..." he moaned, fingers still exploring me, working towards their end goal.

"I'm on the pill," I whispered back, wrapping my legs around his waist and pulling him closer. Feeling the hardness of his long length press against me I had never been more thankful for the painful periods I endured to force me to go on the pill. He groaned with pleasure as he positioned himself, ready to give it all to me. Anticipation and excitement had me on the ropes, pushing me over the edge before the game had even begun.

"Tell me if I hurt you..." he whispered into my ear as I felt his tip enter me, my back arched, wanting more. I felt my world shift, completing, fixing. The things I had become so afraid of was what I now craved the most, what I needed to breathe. "You okay?" he asked, noticing a tear trickle down the side of my face, concern crept over his.

"I'm more than okay," I breathed hoarsely

"I love you, Ana..." he moaned, going deeper, slowly and steady. My breath hitched at his last words, I wanted to say them back but couldn't. Everyone I've ever loved hurts me or leaves me, I would never let him leave. He increased the pace, losing himself in me, taking what he needed and building me up to my ultimate release. He seemed an expert in this subject, his hands and body knew all the right places to touch and kiss as his mouth spilled words picked perfectly for me. I realized then that he was a specialist in everything he did.

Quickly lifting me up, he shifted so he was sat up and I was straddling him, the move so fast I groaned with pleasure. The feel of my Amadore buried deep inside me made my mind race. I couldn't believe how far I had come with his help; how much he had healed me. It was like I had spent my whole life with missing pieces, until now. He had completed me entirely, pulled away all the bad, hurtful memories and slowly replaced them with only thoughts of him.

His eyes had turned dark and hungry as they explored my body and his brows furrowed with what looked like longing and perhaps pain. I could tell - in that moment - he needed me just as much as I needed him. Just the sight of his rippling muscles on his arms and the way his abs moved and pulsed as he slid his length inside me had me quivering on the edge. My enjoyment was too intense as I held his head, kissing him with everything I had. Sliding my tongue in his mouth I claimed him completely. He was all mine. He held my hips as his strong hands gripped onto me, helping me find the rhythm to ride him perfectly.

But it was too much.

I yelled out in blissful pleasure as my relief came quickly and intensely. "Oh, Anabelle..." Amadore moaned, finding his undoing and coming inside me, hot and fast. "so beautiful..." he groaned again, lifting me and laying me back down "Are you okay?" he asked again as he stroked my face, needing reassurance.

"I've never been this happy, Amadore." I replied, still panting as I stole another kiss.

"Neither have I..." he whispered, and I believed him. The evidence was written all over his face. There have been times in my life when I knew, without any doubt, that I had to fight. Had to realize what I want... and take it. Now was one of these times. He was all of me and I needed him more that air. I also knew, with every single fiber of my being, that I would never put him in danger. I would happily die before that happened... and I would die a happy woman... a completed one.

"What now then?" I asked. I felt some sort of game plan to deal with his erratic brothers was probably in order.

"Now..." he thought briefly as he rolled onto his back and wrapped one arm around me, placing the other behind his head. "Now we spend the rest of the night hauled up in this bed." he grinned with sexual intent as my insides did back flips at the thought, "then I'll deal with my charming brothers in the morning." *great.*

"How do we do that?"

"*We* don't do anything... well, we do, but not that. I'll deal with them." his grin was heart-rendering. At times it almost burnt to see it so beautiful.

"I'll come with you then. I won't hide behind you, Amadore." I warned. His brothers will never respect me if they think he's got some little girly, play-toy in tow, I thought. This appeared to make him happy, which in turn... made me ecstatic.

"Okay..." his eyes began to scheme. Thinking up a plan which would get me involved, yet, keep me safe I suppose. "Okay, fine. We'll deal with it tomorrow." he said as he released a puff of air, his tension with it.

"Can I ask you something?" I questioned. I had a million questions about him, and I wanted an answer to every single one. I wanted to know him completely. Every single part.

"Anything."

"How did you come to be... who you are? I mean, like, what you are?" I hoped my question didn't sound as foolish to him as it did to me, but I was intrigued to know his history.

"I've always been this way. I was born like it."

"Like... as a baby...?" I asked as he spluttered with amusement, before gaining control.

"As opposed to..." his heavenly laughter was now breaking up his words "In an egg?" I joined him in side-splitting laughter at what I had just stupidly suggested. It was so strange to be joking about him being born in an egg, yet, he was fifty percent bird. He laughed like he was normal and like I was the odd one. As did I. "Sorry,

sorry..." he breathed through his laughter, fighting to gain control and answer my question. "Yes... a baby." he burst out laughing again, this time a tear streamed down his face. I had to sit up and hold my sides as laughter so loud and exhilarating exploded from my belly. I think I carried on laughing because I had never heard myself laugh like this... happiness was brimming at my surface.

After a good ten minutes of well needed, painful laughter, we finally managed to compose ourselves to have a good chat about his parents and their life. He told me that it was his dad who was a shifter as well. His mother, to my surprise, was just a human girl. I don't know why it made me happy, but it really did. Perhaps, to think it does happen, that heavenly creatures such as Amadore can fall for mere humans like me. I also pried on his older history, asking him such questions as 'who was the first ever shifter?' To which I earned myself a "I don't know... google it." response. We spoke until four thirty in the morning, yet I didn't want to sleep. I just wanted to look at him, hear his voice. Listen to the sound his breathing makes. Watch how his smooth chest rose and fell with his breaths.

"You want to sleep now?" he asked, a smile

giving him away, he was happy too, very happy. Everything he did all seemed so normal, so human. It was easy to forget that just over two hours ago, a bird flew in my window. Just a glance into my superman's eyes and everything else seems to burn to ash. My whole world could disappear behind him and I wouldn't care, as long as he was there.

"No." I answered, gently pushing myself up and sliding my leg over him to leave myself naked and straddling his hard body beneath me.

"Oh, I see... more?" he growled, sending my desire up in fireworks above me

"More..." I whispered back, needing him every second of every day, unsure if I was ever going to stop wanting more of him. All of him.

"I've created a monster... a sexy as fuck, insatiable as all hell - monster" he grinned as I chuckled.

"You only have yourself to blame, Mr. Renato," I swooned as I pushed downwards on him as he slowly entered me again. "But your monster needs feeding... so jump to it." I joked as he laughed, obeying my order, and making love to me for the rest of the night.

Chapter 11

I stretched out in my bed, feeling sore and utterly ravished. My hair was a knotty mess, the sheets were crumpled and the white pillows on the floor. All signs of a very good night with my superman. I could hear music from somewhere as I sat up and yawned, glancing at the clock, midday already. I laughed and fell backwards, touching my lips as I remembered his kisses, my fingers tracing down my neck, following where they went. My grin couldn't stop claiming me, I was so alive, living for one thing. Mr. Amadore Renato. I recognized the song playing, the song from the car, the song he sang so beautifully.

"I'm yours..." I whispered, chuckling at how love struck I was. All my dreams had come true. He made love to me until the birds chirped outside, whispering romantic words all night until the early hours, so gentle and sexy. I glanced over to see a note on my bedside table.

Gone to get clothes, the car and breakfast for my princess, won't be long.

I had the best night of my life, thank you.
Amadore xx

I held it to my chest for a moment, before kissing it and placing it back on the side "I love you, too..." I whispered so quietly, biting my lip.

"You love who?" a voice rang, making me scream and stare wide eyed at the doorway to my bedroom, clutching the sheets to my chest. Katherine, my Mum.

"What the hell?" I scorned "You can't just walk in here like that!" I continued, infuriated.

"I pay for the place so I think I can, actually," her eyes examining the room "However, if I knew it was being used as some sort of sex pad, I might not have been so eager to care for you." she snipped.

"Care for me?" I scoffed "I haven't seen you in three years, mother. And I don't call chucking money at me caring." I snapped, anger raging inside me.

"Me neither." Amadore's voice rang like music as he walked up and squeezed past my mum, perching on the bed next to me. I knew that wherever he was, whatever he was doing- he just heard me scream. That is why he was here at the exact right moment. I fought everything inside me to not smile but I couldn't stop. This was my life now. Protected by the most handsome man on the planet. I still laid naked apart from the sheet and he quickly looked me up and down, a smirk playing on his lips. Memories of last night still playing on his mind too. I was aware of my mother standing in the doorway, yet I was blinded by him. He shrugged his black duffle coat off, revealing a black V-neck sweater, teamed with matching dark blue jeans and smart shoes, his shoulder length hair glossy and beautiful, framing his face. He smelt utterly divine, making my insides tremble enjoyably.

"And, who is this?" she asked, swooning over my man, licking her lips like she could taste his money, fucking bitch.

"This -" I snapped, placing my hand on Amadore's shoulder "Is too young for you, mother." I shot back, earning me a wide eyed expression from my superman, followed by a chuckle, amused at my outburst.

"ANABELLE!" my mother yelled, clearly embarrassed by my statement "Sorry about my daughter, she never learnt manners." she snapped back, then sent a smile Amadore's way.

"Actually, Anabelle is the nicest person I know," my superman said, resting his hand on my knee. "Would you like me to see you out, Mrs. Jones?" he offered, still remaining calm and polite.

"Find out what she's here for first." I spoke quietly, so quietly only he would hear. He looked at me with narrow eyes, working out what I had meant, then rose to his feet and stood directly in front of my mother. The air changed as everything shifted to my mum, then moved so his eyes were all she could see, mesmerized, unable to look away.

"*The real reason you are here, Katherine. Tell me now.*" his voice was deadly, and sexy as hell, you would be forgiven for just doing what he said anyway, no mind control needed.

"Anabelle's father has been released from prison. I was seeing if he had stopped by. I need to get in contact." Her eyes were glazed over, lost in Amadore's. He seemed pained for a moment, staring deeply into Katherine's eyes, reading her completely, getting the truth. His hand clenched, white knuckles shaking, anger spilling over his sides.

"Calm down..." I whispered. It was no surprise how she felt. I knew she hated me for ratting dad in and not 'working through it like a family' so she put it. She had a new, wealthy man whom she spent no time finding when Bill had been put away. But she didn't love him, it was obvious. She loved a child abuser. At times, she was more fucked up than me. What struck me is that he was released well over a year early, he was walking free, God knows where. Visions of him coming for me choked me, fear rising from places I had buried it long ago. When Amadore promised I was in no danger, he was lying. Perhaps not from his kind, but from mine. He would protect me, I knew that like I knew the sun would rise tomorrow, that didn't stop the fear though, the fear of how truly dangerous my father was.

"Leave now, and don't return unless Anabelle invites you." he growled as he broke eye contact, life returned to my mother's eyes as she stood confused for a moment, "Mrs. Jones," Amadore called back "*The key, please.*" he held out his hand as she dropped her key to my flat in his hand.

"Goodbye." she whispered, as she left swiftly.

Amadore was by my side so quickly, cradling me softly and stroking my head, soothing my inner fears as I clung to him. He rubbed his temple, soothing a headache I assumed he got from performing his mind control.

"Don't even worry about it, princess." He assured me "He won't get within a mile of you without me knowing about it." He kissed my forehead, pulling me out of myself, bringing me back down into his arms where I belonged.

"But what if…" I stuttered

"No, no what ifs. You're a lot safer than you realize, I swear it." he interrupted "Do you trust me?" he asked as I nodded and lunged on top of him, wrapping my arms around him and burying my face in his neck.

"I trust you with my life." I confessed, knowing it was true.

"And your naked body, apparently." he chuckled as I peeked down, realizing I was spread over him, still butt-naked. He rolled over, positioning me beneath him as I gazed up into his eyes, his superb features alight and overwhelming. "I brought fresh coffee and muffins, get dressed, princess. Then we'll eat. Then I'm taking you out to spoil you rotten." he gleamed, excited with his plans "Then I'm bringing you back here to have my wicked way with you again."

"Can I spoil you, too?" I asked, needing to give him everything he gives me, needing to please him.

"You spoil me with your company, I need for nothing else"

***

'Spoiling me rotten' was the understatement of the year, we shopped around town for a few hours, anything I like, he bought. No questions asked. Dresses, shoes and of course, he spent the most money in a sexy lingerie store in the mall, lacy numbers in all colors had his eyes turning dark and dangerous.

"Amadore, how are you so rich?" I asked curiously. I never really saw him work, yet judging by his clothes, car and home, he had mountains of cash.

"The jobs I do pay very well," he replied, wrapping his arm around me as we waited in the queue of the smoothie counter.

"What sort of people do you offer your protection to?" I questioned, thinking that it must only be filthy rich celebrities or multimillionaires.

"Anyone who offers the correct amount

for the size of the job."

"What about... say... a criminal wanted protection... to break out of prison?"

"How much is he offering?" he asked, taking me by surprise.

"Seriously? You'd consider that?" I replied, still in shock.

"Not everyone is who you think they are princess. I'd obviously do my research. What if I found out that he was an innocent man trying to break free...?"

"What if he wasn't?" I pressed on.

"Then I don't help."

"Why care for the price then?" he seemed exasperated at my interrogation, yet continued to answer my questions calmly. He very rarely talked about his job before, perhaps I was now finding out why.

"Because if the amount of cash he is offering is worth the risk, I'll do my research to see whether the client is." His response seemed reasonable and I cursed myself inwardly for thinking otherwise of him. Angels like him don't taint this world.

"Is it just shifters that exist then?" I questioned further as he grinned, perhaps pleased with the sudden conversation change.

"What do you mean?"

"What about vampires? And fairies? Or whatever?" he grinned at my question, probably thinking how dumb I was, yet, I thought it was quite a valid one. I mean, if shifters exist - what else does?

"No, princess. No vampires or fairies. There are variations of shifters though... so I've read anyway."

"What does that mean?"

"It's heard of, although it's very rare, that people who have powers, but without the shifter gene, exist. I've never met anyone myself, but apparently one of my cousins have. He met a man who could read minds, like properly." I loved how he told me things so easily, like he trusted me entirely. It warmed me to the core just listening to his words and how he spoke them, all the time watching my reaction, "but there is a whole array of different types, like healers, people who can talk to animals, people who see the future, people who walk in dreams and some just have small threads of power, who would appear totally normal, but are not."

"Like how?"

"For example, someone might think that they just get their own way a lot, but actually they use tiny amounts of mind control, they just don't know it."

"Have you ever used your powers in other ways?" I whispered so that everyone around couldn't hear, grinning up at him.

"I would be lying if I said no. When I was younger and more stupid... like Carlos is now." he grinned back.

"I noticed you got a headache earlier, was that because of mind control? I mean, does it hurt?"

"Sometimes..." he paused for a moment, seeming to think about his response "Some people are harder to manipulate than others."

"What about me?" I asked, curiosity simmering in my belly.

"You're a fighter, you take to it but your brain battles back." He grinned, running his hand down my cheek. I felt sort of smug, I'm a fighter... yeah, right.

"Do you age like normal people?" I pressed on, remembering all the questions I wanted to know answers to.

"Yes, my flesh and blood is just like

everyone else's. I heal quicker… a lot quicker and turn into a bird, of course, but I grow and age, yes. You finished?" he asked humorously. Enjoying the light in my eyes that glowed just for him, captivated by his words and how he spoke them. Passing me my smoothie we slowly strolled hand in hand, heading to the spa to continue my pampering.

"How do you die then?" I asked, still intrigued

"Why? You trying to kill me off?" he laughed, always so happy and carefree. I blushed and shook my head "It's my bones that make me strong, but my heart could give way as any other eighty-year-old man. Obviously, I can be killed too." he thought for a moment "But they would have to have some major skills," he winked at me, just the thought of him being killed made me panicky. I squeezed his hand tight and stopped walking, instead choosing to wrap my arms around him, kissing him passionately before pulling away, remember another question I wanted to ask.

"Last night… you were worried about… erm… protection. Does that mean…?" a sweeping grin overcame his face, his eyes suddenly very amused watching me struggle with my next question "Help me out, please." I laughed as I looked down, my cheeks flushing awkwardly.

"My little soldiers are in full working order, yes." he placed his finger under my chin, pulling my gaze up to meet his, smiling profoundly.

"And children that you might have... will they be...?" I fought, wanting to know answers but the questions were humiliating, I secretly prayed he knew my reasons for asking and didn't think I wanted to start trying for babies.

"Depends on who the mother is. If I was to have... I don't know... a baby with you- for example, there would be a fifty percent chance he... or she would be a shape shifter like me... like my parents did... and obviously if two shape shifters conceive, they would most definitely have a shifter," I recalled the conversation we had last night and kicked myself for not remembering sooner... that would have perhaps saved me the embarrassment of this particular conversation. "Done now?" he asked as he leant down and kissed me and in that moment the world faded around us. By the time we pulled away to breathe we noticed we were causing quite the scene. "Let's get going," Amadore grinned as he whispered in my ear, kissing my forehead delicately before dragging me off to get my hair and nails done.

***

"I really don't know about this anymore, Amadore" I sat nervously in the Jag as we once again headed up his long driveway, descending on his mansion full of big, strong (and pretty fucking mean) shape shifters. I looked down and tugged at my green wrap dress, pulling it over my knees. The last thing I want is his brothers to think I was easy as well as a danger hazard.

"Don't pick." Amadore warned, talking about the fact I had my nails done a little under an hour ago, and my nerves were already forcing me to take it out on the beautiful handy work of the nail technician. "I wouldn't bring you back here to throw you to the wolf, I promise." he tried to assure me, but didn't succeed. I knew I had asked for this, knew that this is what I wanted. Yet, it was sort of easy to talk all brave from the confounds of my safe little room... Shit just got real now.

Amadore parked the car and appeared at the passenger door in seconds, undoing my seat belt for me and taking my hand, helping me out.

"Breathe," he reminded me as I sucked in a

big breath.

"Don't let them kill me, please." I pleaded, only half joking.

"Bernardo, we're here." he said, looking towards the door as it opened.

"Oh, Christ." I cursed, looking down at my new Mary-Jane shoes, wishing I decided on my flats, in case I needed to run... not that I could escape a wolf, let alone a super speedy shape shifter. I peeked up through my eyelashes and squeezed my superman's hand as Bernardo strolled up to us.

"Anabelle, I think we may have got off on the wrong foot before... I'm Bernardo." the growl to his voice still echoed as I realized that was just how he sounded, angry or not.

"Hello, Bernardo." my voice shaken and feeble, almost non-existent.

"Please, accept my apology." he said, sounding genuine as he held out his hand. I took my trembling hand from Amadore's and placed it in Bernardo's, shaking his as I smiled. I dared a glance at Amadore who was stood, somewhat pleased with himself. In that moment I had a sneaky suspicion that he perhaps had already dealt with this problem like he said he was going to... I wanted to feel angry at him for not letting me be involved... but I wasn't. In fact, I was glad. Bernardo is a lot scarier than I had remembered.

"You have no reason to apologize." I said, my voice sounding a lot more confident than I felt "Its lovely to meet you."

"I see why my brother is so charmed by you now, please - come in." I was somewhat grateful that perhaps one person could see why Amadore was so charmed, as I hadn't a clue, perhaps he could enlighten me one day, I thought. Following through the huge front door, the house was stunning. I was instantly taken aback by the grand staircase and shiny wooden banisters, the stairs veered off leading to what I could only imagine to be the left and right wings of the house. Huge arched door frames opened up to other rooms, all decorated delicately with old art work. Antique rugs laid on the shiny wooden floor boards, I glanced up at the magnificent glass chandelier hanging high above the stairs.

"Wow..." I whispered as Amadore pressed himself up against my back, wrapping his arms around my waist.

"You like?" he asked, biting my ear lobe.

"It's incredible..." I swooned, too lost for

words to elaborate. Stunned to silence, the house only confirmed what I already knew, Amadore was a God.

"Anabelle..." I heard a voice to the left as I turned, Watching Carlos appear from some kind of giant lounge area "Let's start again, shall we? I'm Carlos." he held out his hand as I quickly did too, shaking it as relief flooded over me, this was all going quite well. Carlos looked more like Amadore than Bernardo did, except younger. He was completely clean shaven and his short hair the same color as my superman, just spiky and boyish.

"Nice to meet you, Carlos." I replied warmly, taking in his appearance. His dress sense screamed money, I assumed that was how he wanted to be perceived. His smart Armani suit and Rolex told me all I needed to know, he loved his life... and himself.

"Like the suit?" he asked, watching my eyes examine him.

"Better than you being naked I suppose." I joked, making Amadore chuckle.

"Oh, you don't mean that."

"I like the puppy the best though," I said with a giggle

"I get that a lot, from women mostly." his eyes were playful, enjoying the banter.

"Wait until he gets older, he'll be a fully grown Labrador. No more peeking up girls' skirts, hey bro?" Amadore joined in, grinning the whole time.

"But tall enough to sniff crotches." Carlos shot back, making me and my superman grimace at his joke which perhaps crossed a line.

"You'll get used to his sick sense of humor, princess." Amadore laughed, although it seemed he was still yet to warm to it.

"Anyway, nice to see you. Got to go, ladies to…" he paused to think of the word he wanted "Meet? Yeah… we'll go with 'meet'. Rude to say 'fuck' in front of guests." Carlos grinned, sending a wink my way before waving and heading out of the front door, leaving my superman shaking his head in exasperation.

"He seems… playful." I chose my words carefully

"You could say that." Amadore replied.

"I didn't know your animals age with you?" I continued, intrigued by this new piece of information.

"Of course. They're not *our* animals…

they are us." he explained, making it seem so obvious "The older we get the abler we are at sensing one another too." he added, slipping me more things to ask about, more things I needed to know.

"What do you mean?"

"For example, a young shape shifter could walk right past me and it would merely make me turn my head. However, I can tell you if an old one is within two miles of us. The older we get, the more our powers stand out to others like us." he grinned at me as I listened intently, fascinated by him "You want to stand here and chat all evening? Or do you want to see the sights?"

"Oh, yeah..." I remembered where I was and smiled back "Let's see the sights now, we'll talk about this later?"

"Sure," he replied as he took my hand, leading me up the stairs. I walked slowly, running my fingers up the banister with awe, breathing in the smells of polish and perhaps something cooking in the kitchen. I felt like a princess as he reached the top of the stairs and turned to watch me follow him, gleaming at me like his prize.

"We'll be here all day if you're going to walk around in a dream world like that." he joked, still smiling.

"I am in a dream world, aren't I?" I shot back, grinning delightfully

"No, princess. You're in my world now." He lifted me up the last step, swooping me into his arms and began carrying me down a long corridor. Giant oak doors sat either side and a royal red carpet hugged the floor. He headed towards the door at the very end, placing me down as we reached it and kissing me on the forehead "After you," he said as I placed my hand on the door knob, turning it gently.

Chapter 12

The room was bigger than my whole apartment and was absolutely breath-taking. The ceiling sat high up and decorative swirls swept dreamily in the aertex towards the chandelier. I instantly noticed the giant window which fell from the ceiling to the floor on my left, light shone in like from heaven to earth, a brown leather lounge sofa sat facing out of it, books scattered on top and on the polished wooden floor. My eyes worked their way round to the right. A wooden fire place centered the room, also seeming larger than life as fire blazed, warming the room. I felt a smile on my face, one I couldn't help. Other old fashioned decorations finalized the room, a bookshelf full of old looking novels, a grand piano, three acoustic guitars, a throw and scatter cushioned placed in the right hand corner added a cozy relaxation area, perhaps for reading or playing his instruments. I stared for a moment at an old looking trunk which sat in the corner and made a mental note to have a peek inside later.

"What do you think?" he asked examining my face for approval, I walked inside towards the piano, tapping a few keys as I beamed

"Almost as stunning as you." I bit my lip,

sure I would wake up from this dream. I thought about how safe I was here, surely it would take one hell of an army to get past three shape shifting Gods. I chuckled, my thoughts amusing me "You play this?" I asked, still prodding the keys.

"Not really, a little. I'm more attached to my guitar," he replied walking over to the throw on the floor and sitting down, leaning back on his elbows and crossing his legs, watching me stroll over to the window, which was well over twice my height. The view was breathtaking, just fields and trees as far as the eye could see, country side at its most absolute. The sky was getting darker as the time rolled on to almost five and pink clouds streaked over the sky. Hearing his strings pluck beautifully on his guitar I turned, my feet walked towards him instinctively, kneeling down in front of him, he glanced up, a smile playing on the corners of his lips.

"Play something for me..." I asked him. His face turned serious as he looked down to his guitar, beginning to pluck and strum at the strings, so beautifully. I laid down, resting my head on the pillows, letting the tune leak out of him and embrace my soul. It was then his voice began to sing, so beautiful, so pained, it was all so magnificent a tear rolled down my cheek.

"Morning pours across the sky...
Thoughts of you invade my shore...
I turn and you are by my side...
My greatest wish- could not give me more..."

I opened my eyes and met his gaze, his eyes seemed loving and passionate, he plucked out his heavenly music as my breath hitched and I rested my weight on my elbows, needing to get the perfect view of the best moment of my life.
"Please forgive me if I'm staring...
When your eyes awake to face the day...
It's just when you're out of sight...
I need your image to always stay...

My angel, I want...
To be strong like you...
Fight after fight and yet...
Your strength simply shines straight through...
You caress me with your smile...
Melt my heart with words you say...

And when you hold me in your eyes...

I'm in my tender time of day...

Oh, Angel...

You are my tender time of day..."

My...oh...my. He strummed out the final notes, a smile playing at the side of his lips. I laid still, unable to move or speak, so overwhelmed, so in love. He finished and placed his guitar to the side, crawling over next to me and lying down, placing his hand on my face and sliding it into my hair.

"Anyone... I have ever loved... has hurt me... or left." I stuttered, my voice shaken and fearful, yet so... so in love.

"Is that your way of telling me you love me, princess?" his half grin calmed me, pulling the words out of me.

"Yes, I suppose it is." I was beginning to feel lust once more, a need to please him making my insides quiver with anticipation, with desire for him.

"That look you're giving me right now... do I need to take you home?" his gaze turned dark, like he read my mind.

"No...here is just fine." I growled, my voice husky, heavy with pleasure. Amadore laughed at something which was apparently funny, confusion creased between my brow "Did I say something funny?" I asked.

"No, but Bernardo said to take this elsewhere." he laughed again as my face flushed bright red.

"Oh yeah, sorry..." I planted my face in my hand feeling so ashamed

"Let's get out of here." Amadore swooped me up into his arms "Hold on tight... and close your eyes." he whispered as my grip tightened, but my eyes stayed open, I couldn't see anything apart from my hair which was blowing over my face and flashes of color shooting past. I couldn't breathe either, it was like sticking your head out of a speeding car window, then we stopped outside the car door, as I glanced around.

"Impressive." I swooned as he nodded once

"Hop in," he opened the door to the Jag "I need to get you home now."

****

We fell through my front door, tearing at each other's clothes and kissing intensely, his tongue dipped into my mouth, teasing me. Edging me forward, closer to him, I groaned with pleasure as with one quick swoop he pulled my dress over my head and left me stood in just my heels and matching black lacy underwear. He lunged at me, unable to cover up his lust and reached down to cup my rear, lifting me so my legs wrapped around his waist. One second we were stood by my door then we were on the bed, he peeled off his sweater as I fumbled with his fly, I hadn't managed it as he forced me backwards and began kissing down my stomach.

"Oh... Amadore," I purred, running my hands through his hair.

"Your heart beats so loud for me..." he moaned back as he began to pull at my underwear, his kisses pressing delicately at my hip. His mouth licking and biting, teasing my senses. I was about to tell him I loved him, I knew that right now, in the mist of our lust for one another, was the perfect time. I wanted him to know that I trusted him, that I loved him more than life. Instead I was silenced instantly as he sat up, fear injected like heroin in his eyes as he slammed his hand over my mouth.

"It's your father... he's here... should I kill him?"

Chapter 13

I slammed my hand over top of Amadore's as a scream reached my throat, he laid topless over of me, his eyes glaring at the doorway to my bedroom. His hair framing his face and his eyes wild with anger.

"Should I kill him?" he whispered again, but my eyes stayed wide and penetrated with fear. What was he doing here? Had he come back to punish me for going to the police? for ending his two-year torture he forced on to me? ruining my childhood entirely. "It's OK, look at me, Anabelle." I allowed my eyes to meet his "Do as I say, ok?" he insisted, but I couldn't, I was frozen with fear and dread. He slowly moved his hand away "You can do this."

"No... I can't." I couldn't think straight, my mind whirled around like a hurricane as I gasped for air "Make me... make me do what you need, please." I begged, knowing the only way I was going to cooperate was to be completely unaware I was, I needed him to make me forget. His eyes turned quickly, drawing me in and I felt myself shift, there was nothing anymore, nothing but his eyes, everything I ever knew laid there.

"I'm sorry princess, remember that. I'm going to go to the car, I have forgotten something... you would like a hot shower, and you won't come out of the bathroom 'till I come and fetch you... remain calm, nothing bad is happening, it's just me and you here." I felt my mind return as Amadore hopped out of bed and shot out of the room. My mind felt blurry, fighting its way through the truth and the lies. Confusion had me hooked. *You're a fighter... stop fighting it...* I heard my mind scorn me. I needed a shower, I knew that much. I hopped out of bed, grabbing some clean pajama bottoms and a vest. Deciding to strip off and hop in the shower... and perhaps wait for Amadore to come join me, my insides delighted with the idea of getting him in the shower, all hot and wet. I chuckled under my breath as I headed into the bathroom.

Standing under the hot water was cleansing and relaxing, that was until gunshots made me scream. I jumped out of the shower, tugging my clothes on over my wet body, running to the door and grabbing the door handle. *open the door...* I willed myself, but I couldn't turn it. Not because it was locked but because my hand just wouldn't. *Amadore, what have you done?...* I knew my mind wasn't letting me leave, and as he is the only one with the power to control it, he had to be up to something. I remembered that he was sorry... but why? He left something in the car... didn't he? I felt drips of water from my hair trickle down my back.

"AMADORE!" I yelled out, knowing he would hear and began banging on the door. "AMADORE, PLEASE!" I called once more as the door knob rattled. I stepped back and watched it open, coming face to face with my father... who was covered in blood and grinning devilishly.

I remembered instantly as I began to sob, I should have stayed quiet, instead I chose to sign my own death warrant.

"Where's Amadore?" I whimpered feeling eleven again, asking for my soft toy to hold so I could feel comfort while he abused me. He saw it too. His old haggard face glared at me, his grey eyes peering at me in the way they did, the way I'll never understand. His brown hair had more grey in it than I remembered, and was messy and distressed. He lunged at me, grabbing my wrist and began dragging me out, hauling me towards the door as I kicked and punched, but he was strong... incredibly strong, I remembered now why I never fought back seven years ago, there was no point, there never was. It was seeing Amadore's body, blood soaked and lying motionless on the rug on the floor which brought an ear piercing scream to my mouth as I shook uncontrollably.

"NO! AMADORE!! WAKE UP!!" I screeched, trying to run towards him as my dad yanked me back

"Shut up you stupid little slut, his brothers will hear," yes, I thought, yes they would.

"BERNARDO!!" I yelled with everything in me "CARLOS!!" I yelled again, as my father's fist rained down on my face and darkness took me.

****

The bumps in the road jolted me back to consciousness and my head banged on the metal floor of the van I was caged in. I could feel the swelling round my eyes, forcing me to keep them shut. I gently lifted my head and placed my hand on my temple, attempting to relieve the ache which banged on the inside of it.

Amadore...

Tears welled in my eyes instantly as the sight of him came crashing back to me. He wasn't dead. He couldn't be...

If he was... I wished to die too.

"Morning." the terrifying voice of my fathers echoed as I finally peeled my eyes open. He was sat in the driver's seat, peering at me in the mirror. "Didn't mean to punch you that hard... Thought I broke your neck!" he laughed as I turned away. Anger rose up into my throat making me want to scream, but I didn't. I would never again give him the satisfaction of seeing any of my emotions... He no longer owned them. Amadore did.

I shuffled my way down to the doors of the van, knowing I would get a reaction and began kicking them violently, desperate for them to fly open so I could run.

"STOP THAT!" Bill yelled, only making me kick harder. My bare feet felt numb as I continued my onslaught. It didn't hurt, nothing did. Not without my superman. "THAT'S IT!" He yelled again, slamming on the breaks hard sending my body hurdling down the van smashing my head on the floor.

The darkness was wanted. It was better than living. It was better than breathing. I had spent three perfect weeks praying I wouldn't wake up from my dream with Amadore... now I begged to God as I slept. Begged him to wake me from this nightmare.

Chapter 14

My head...hurt...so bad. I rolled over, feeling cold, dirty concrete underneath me. I went to touch my head to inspect the damage, to realize my hands were shackled together, I pulled on them to hear a chain tighten. I managed to open one eye and look up. They were chained to the wall. I lifted up my head and looked around. From the glow of the candle which shone in the corner I could just see brick walls, nothing else. No windows and only one door. I began to sob, praying death would take me sooner rather than later. If Amadore was dead, I wanted to be too. I had nothing worth living for if I didn't have him. The thought of him dying whilst trying to save me overcame me and I sobbed louder and harder. I must have laid there for hours, not fighting or even moving. Just crying my heart out of my eyes.

"My angel, I want to be strong like you..." I sobbed to myself, my voice breaking as I recalled his song to me, remembering how our evening was supposed to end. I was shocked as light suddenly beamed through the doorway and a dark figure stood in the way, I couldn't see who it was, but he just stood there staring at me.

"Help me..." I sobbed, praying for a miracle. Praying that even if the person wasn't here to save me, he would be here to kill me, to end me now.

"Anabelle, you silly girl," my father's voice droned, making me shuffle away and pull at my restraints "What can I do to punish you sufficiently?"

"...Go fuck yourself," I whimpered back, not sounding even half as threatening as it was supposed to "Fuck you!" I tried again, succeeding.

"Watch your language, you little slut!" he cursed at me, taking a step into the room. And going to close the door.

"Bill?" I heard my mother say, as hope pricked in my belly.

"MUM!" I cried out as she entered too "Mum! Help!" I yelled again, sobbing profusely, I was saved, I had to be. She went to walk towards me as Bill stopped her and glared into her eyes "Anabelle has been very bad and she needs to be punished... go fix the dinner, I'll deal with her." mums eyes were dead as she turned and walked away.

"Mind control..." I watched my mum disappear through the door as everything clicked into place "You're... a shape shifter..." I whispered.

"Oh, look at you. You find yourself a little boyfriend who turns into a fucking bird and now you're a master of the subject!" he spat. My mum never believed me because she couldn't, she had no choice... I felt for my mother in that moment, she probably had never made a decision on her own in the last twenty-one years, he would have made it for her. Choosing what he wanted her to do, then making her do it.

"Why... Why let me remember? Why not just tell me to forget? You would have never been caught?" I had no idea what I was asking and why I felt the need to put ideas into his head, but I needed closure, needed to understand.

"What? And not getting to see that pretty little face of yours, all frightened and alone," he enlightened me... he never made me forget because he was a sick, twisted, son of a bitch "Plus, you can't perform mind control over blood relatives, didn't prince charming tell you that?" his snide comment irritated me, just him getting to speak of Amadore made me angry.

"He knew you were coming though, you dirty old bastard." I snapped back as realization hit home. Amadore knew he wasn't running to defend me against a pathetic human. He knew he was coming because he sensed him, he sensed an old shape shifter. My superman knew... even before I did. Tears welled behind my eyes as I thought. How long had he known? Did he work it out as he sensed him minutes before... or was he on high alert because he already knew? Bill's eyes were watching me as my mind ran away with thoughts so I changed the subject, not wanting to give him any satisfaction

"Then why do jail time... if you could just tell the judge you're innocent, and he would have believed you?" I questioned further, slightly aware that keeping a conversation going, fair be it - a fucked up conversation, was buying me time before he thought of an appropriate punishment.

"You think I went to a jail full of petulant human low lives like you and your mother?" he shot, spitting anger, "You, you little whore, happened to stumble across one of very few shifting police officers, luckily for you, he sensed you," he shook his head, recalling the day he was dragged out of our home, mum screaming and crying "I've been in a high security prison... for talented folks like myself," he sneered, looking pleased with himself. Bill's words spoke more to me than he realized. The police officer who ran up to me and offered to help on that fateful day had sensed *me*. I wanted to ask him how, but I couldn't. I didn't want him thinking I was uneducated when it came to Amadore, to shape shifting. I wanted Bill to think I knew all about his little game, even though it was becoming more and more apparent I did not. What was also now very clear was my superman saw me coming. Was he there that evening to rescue a mere human girl or had he sensed me too? Was the reason I felt so drawn to him, how I was able to give all myself to him... how I needed him badly, more than air... That I could sense him too... Surely not. I wasn't a shape shifter too...was I?

"AMADORE!!" I yelled at the top of my lungs, aware the door was still open, increasing my chances of him hearing. Bill flew across the room, wrapping his hard, brittle hand across my mouth.

"He is dead, stupid girl," he scowled, straightening himself up, and removing his hand from my mouth to clasp my chin, forcing me to look at him.

I felt anger rise, he wasn't dead. I knew that. He promised I would never be hurt again, that I was in no danger. I still believed that with every part of myself. He would never break them promises, I knew he was coming for me, like I knew Bill would die as soon as he did.

"Then why can't I scream for him, Bill? If he is dead? because you're a liar! that's why! You twisted, self-obsessed, pathetic... cunt." I growled the last word, as I shuffled to my knees, the highest my shackles would allow, taking the blow from his fist dead on, happy to settle in my darkness once more.

His face was so beautiful, just as I had remembered, smiling down at me as he thrust gently inside me "So beautiful..." so swooned, leaning down to kiss me deeply. Our naked bodies connected on multiple levels, fixing each other, healing each other. His fingertips tickled my skin, leaving me breathless and greedy for him, every inch of him.

"Kill my dad, Superman..." I whispered to him as his eyes turned dark and dangerous

"I've done that already, princess..." he growled as he thrust into me again whilst leaving a trail of kisses down my neck. Yes, he had. I remembered. He ripped his head clean off his shoulders. I peered around quickly, noticing his bedroom walls, his silk sheets, his new four poster bed.

"Am I safe now?" I whispered, as Amadore stilled and looked down at me, his face serious for a moment before smiling warmly.

"What do you think? Do you feel safe?" he questioned, playing with my emotions. Of course I was safe, the feel of him inside me told me everything, answered everything, he saved me. He always saves me. His muscular arms either side of my head, protecting me, all hot and sweaty, bulging just for me. I thrust my hips forward, edging him on to continue his slow and sensual display of lust and love.

"Make love to me... forever." I whispered as he groaned with delight.

"My pleasure...." he replied.

I groaned and tried to roll over, quickly becoming alert to the fact that I was torn from my dream by being held still, as my instincts kicked in I tried to screamed but a hand was grasped over my mouth, panic snatched me as I tried to struggle free, I opened my eyes and blinked through my tears... and fell deadly still. I was staring up at

Carlos Renato's beautiful golden eyes, he placed a finger over his mouth and shook his head, silently warning me not to make a noise. I nodded, suddenly feeling empowered and hopeful. He took his hand away from my mouth and grabbed my shoulders, lifting me up to a sitting position

"Wh..." I began as Carlos slammed his hand back over my mouth, shaking his head furiously, glaring at me with angry gold eyes, a little too cute and puppy like to display how angry he probably was, then performing a 'ZIP-IT' gesture, making me fight the smile that was playing on my lips. His cute auburn hair flopped over his head, and he was dressed all in black, looking like the cutest little sneaky spy. I couldn't stop my thoughts drifting to Amadore, where was he? Why wasn't he here? I dismissed the idea that he was hurt, or worse yet, dead. Surely if I caused his brother to die, Carlos wouldn't be here right now, slowly bending the metal shackles around my wrists as I pulled my hands free. I tried to keep my breathing normal so even if Bill was listening, he wouldn't suspect anything.

He placed his finger to his lips, reminding me to stay quiet before signing to me to follow him. He was crouching over as he snuck to the door, opening it with stealth, and peering down the hall before holding out his hand to me. Hope suddenly fluttered in my stomach as I remembered a conversation Amadore and I had. Carlos was here because he was the hardest to sense, he was young. I couldn't help my hopes from rising, hoping that somewhere, outside these revolting brick walls was my superman, ready to hold me, to take me home. Sneaking with bare feet was pretty easy, and holding Carlos's hand filled me with confidence. *just do what he says* my conscience told me *do what he says and you get to live.* Carlos squeezed my hand gently, and offered me a sympathetic grin. I dreaded to think of how my face looked after the two hefty punches I had received from Bill. Judging by Carlos's expression, I was sensing I didn't look great. As we crept into the long hallway I noticed that the house I was in was unrecognizable, yet, compared to the dark, dirty basement I was held in it looked warm, homely. The floors were coated in a clean, beige carpet that felt comfortable under my feet. The walls were coated in fresh magnolia paint and images of sunsets and beach scenes decorated them. I wondered briefly if this was Katherine's and Bill's new home. Where they are planning their 'happily-ever-after' with their traitorous daughter, locked up never to be found. I grinned as I wondered if they had even thought about the three brothers who would undoubtedly come for me.

My feet padded as quietly as they could down the corridor as I clung tightly to Carlos's hand, he moved without a sound ahead of me, his ears and eyes working overtime. I had so many questions to ask him. Where was Amadore? Is he ok? Why aren't we running? Where are we? I knew I had to stay quiet, I trusted him with my life in this moment, knowing that whatever was happening, whatever his plans, I was safer here- with him- than I was locked away, taking beatings from Bill.

"Where the fuck do you think you're going?" Bill cursed from behind us, but before I could react, Carlos grabbed me and ran, I couldn't see anything, just color flashing past my face, it got cold as we headed to what I assumed was outside,

"We're busted!" Carlos yelled as he halted and placed me on wet grass. I frantically looked around, I could see the delicate cottage I was imprisoned in, a dirt road leading from it to the unknown. Bernardo growled loudly, preparing to battle as Carlos joined him. Bill burst out of the door at that moment, loading a shotgun and swearing loudly as he realized Carlos hadn't come alone. He was already poised and geared up, Bernardo next to him, edging forward - ready to attack. My eyes searched desperately, then froze. Next to his brothers, Amadore was stood, ready to kill.

Chapter 15

"You are supposed to be dead!" Bill yelled, fury making him shake uncontrollably as he stalked forward, all three brothers poised and ready. The grass was wet and cold under my bare feet and the sky was black and crystal clear. The moonlight lit the battlefield for the man I loved more than life versus the man I hated with every inch of myself. I knew that one of them was to lose their life tonight. I also knew who I would bet my money on. My eyes locked onto Amadore. In this moment, he was my air I breathed in. My savior. My hero. I knew my face was bloodied, bruised and swollen, I knew my clothes were dirty and torn. I had nothing to offer him, nothing to give away. Just me. Broken, battered me. But I was his, all his. Although the most part of me would never understand why he would want me. He did. For that alone, it made everything worthwhile. It made fighting seem necessary, because if things were the other way round - I would fight, even kill, for his safety.

"Sorry to disappoint, sir," Amadore growled "But sadly for you, you seemed to have stolen something that belongs to me." Superman shot, his eyes never leaving Bill, so focused and determined.

"She is mine, my daughter." Bill looked from one brother, to another, to another. He was well out of his league and he knew it, I would imagine Bernardo's muscle weighed more than Bills entire body weight.

"In that case, I'm here to steal what's yours." a vindictive grin scorched Amadore's face, wanting to anger my father. I sensed Bill sizing him up before cocking his gun. I stood, my legs shaky and my mind disorientated, staring down at my filthy white vest and pajamas which were distressed and torn at the knees, I was too, well out of my league.

"Never..." he scorned as a deadly promise drenched his words. It seemed in that moment- in a crazy, screwed up way- He needed me. "You may wish to tell my daughter why you're so pulled towards her... because even she knows that you wouldn't fall for a stupid human girl." Bill added, grinning at Amadore's scowl.

"She is human..."my superman snarled through gritted teeth as Bill bellowed a menacing laugh.

"Bill... can you quit the small talk so they

can kill you already... I'm bored." I scorned as he gazed at me, his eyes displaying something that looked like hurt. To distract him briefly was my aim, and it worked. The Renato's saw their opening and took it. Speeding towards my Father, intending to kill and dismantle (I hoped).

    Carlos went for the gun, snatching it and launching it in the air, out of reach as Amadore speared him down. I saw his speed and how deadly he could be in that moment, Bill threw punches with all his might, but my superman blocked and dodged them with ease before landing some hefty blows of his own.

    "End him!" Bernardo ordered, his voice echoing over the fields behind us. A small part of me thought of stopping them. He was my Father, after all. But the biggest part of me wanted to watch. I wanted to see him die. Die painfully and tragically. I put my hand to my mouth to disguise the cry I made, memories flooding back, my small, fragile body being violated in so many ways, so many times. Him destroying my toys, trashing my bedroom, anything that made me happy, he took. And now, for all of that, my superman, what made me happier than anything in this world, would take his life in return. I wondered if he now regretted destroying my favorite doll, or burning my favorite diary, because karma is a bitch and now he has to deal with my favorite man. A man so powerful and strong, with animalistic skills and dangerous reasons to cause damage. My superman would get my revenge for me. I finally had something worth fighting for, and in turn, he would fight for me. Blow after blow rained down on Bill's face as Amadore lost control, his fury radiated, needing Bill to pay "NOW" Bernardo ordered again.

    Amadore launched toward Bill again as Carlos assisted him, all three brothers seemed focused, almost in sync with one other, like they could read each other's mind. I stood in awe as I watched them pin Bill to the floor, my mind went into overload, begging it to be over now. I watched helplessly in spite of myself, I didn't want to see anyone die, anyone killed. But I couldn't look away. That was until a gust of wind sent all three brothers and then myself flying backwards.

    I knew in my head I didn't want to look, in fact, I wanted to stand and run. To just keep running until I physically can't. It was the roar of the giant American black bear which made me turn my head in fear. Amadore was already on his feet, poised to battle and sometime in the mist of this madness, Bernardo had shifted also. The black wolf was much smaller than the bear, yet, I could guarantee he would be faster... I hoped.

Carlos rose back to his feet as a laugh escaped him. There was nothing I could think of that could possibly be funny at this exact moment in time. However, I could imagine Carlos was the type to laugh seconds before he died. He lived for the danger.

"So, what's the plan now?" he asked as Amadore stalked around, looking almost as animalistic as Bernardo in wolf form.

"He still dies..." was all Amadore offered as he launched forward again, this time receiving a hefty blow from a giant claw. I couldn't watch anymore. Amadore's body landing on the ground told me all I needed to know.

Now was the time to help.

I scurried to me feet and quietly began running in the direction to which the gun was thrown. Unlucky for me, Carlos had quite the throw on him, so I had to run further than I thought. My feet were cold and wet as they powered over the muddy ground, but they never gave way.

I stood a fair distance away as my eyes

searched erratically over the ground, desperately needing to see the gun, to take it to Carlos... or perhaps use it myself. A wolf's cry had me covering my ears and choking on my sobs *Please, God. Help me.* I thought with everything in me.

Just then, I caught sight of the shotgun.

Hidden between two tall trees, I rushed over and grabbed it then began my sprint back. I didn't know what I'd do when I got there or how this would help. I couldn't just sit and watch though. It was worth a try.

"DAD!" I yelled as I ran back into the open space where they all fought. Bernardo was back as himself and holding his side as he watched his two brothers duck and dive with the bear. His eyes locked onto mine as I appeared. It was almost like he was trying to tell me something, trying to tear into my mind.

Cause a distraction... I thought to myself as I yelled again.

"Bill... you mother-fucker!" I don't know if it was my words or the fact that I chose to cock the gun at the same time that made him look, but he did. I pointed the gun and stared down the barrel, hoping and praying I wouldn't have to pull the trigger.

With a strong swipe of his huge paw he knocked both Amadore and Carlos flying into Bernardo.

As he bounded towards me I had only one thought.

Amadore.

He was, and always will be, prepared and ready to die for me, as I would him. If my death caused a distraction so that he could live, then so be it.

I took a deep breath in as Bill's footsteps rattled the ground. I could feel all three brothers staring at me as I closed my eyes... and pulled the trigger.

In the instant, I thought it was the recoil of the shotgun which sent me backwards with force, but opening my eyes I saw that wasn't true.

It was Bill, shifting back, bullet wound and all, as the Renato's jumped in. All three diving on him and holding him to the floor.

"It's not the end!" I heard Bill cry as Amadore pinned him down with Carlos, Bernardo placing both hands either side of his neck "I'll be back!" were his final words to me, as I stood a fair distance away, hand still clutched to the gun, trying to digest what I was seeing.

"We'll look forward to it, old man." Amadore stared deep into his eyes, his farewell words intimidating and menacing. The rip and then crack of Bill's neck breaking was so loud it made me drop the shotgun and put my hands over my ears as Bernardo tugged and pulled, beheading him. My eyes instinctively looked away, I had never seen a dead body before, let alone a headless one. Knowing my father was dead was enough, I didn't need more mental images of him.

The next thing I heard was my mother's cry, a scream of pure terror. I looked round but I could not see her anywhere.

"Amadore..." I called to him as he appeared by my side.

"Now he is dead, she remembers... she remembers everything..." he answered my silent question "what would you like me to do?" he asked, reaching up to touch my face then changing his mind, moving his hand away. It was then I noticed his eyes, so hurt, so lost.

"Make her forget," I said, knowing that stealing her memories away was the only thing we could do "Make her remember good things...

picnics in the park, day trips to the beach... make her memories consist of just me and her... like Bill never existed."

"On it!" Carlos called out, heading back into the house to find my mother as I grabbed Amadore's arm.

"Don't." he shot, pulling his arm away from me "I failed you, I don't deserve you."

Really? Really?

After the day I have just had, mostly consisting of lying in a dank, dark basement, taking punches to the face whilst dreaming of him and he now had the balls to deny me of the one thing I needed more than air? I don't fucking think so.

"Oh, no. No you don't. Snap the fuck out of it, superman." Amadore's eyes shot open, amusement playing on the sides of his eyes like the smile playing on the sides of his lips "In case you're forgetting something- that was my dad- so regardless of whether I was in your life or not, he was always going to come back after me. Luckily for me, I did know you, therefore - I'm still alive. So screw you and your 'I failed you' bullshit. You just saved my fucking life. Hold me, God damn you!"

Amadore grabbed me, wrapping two

strong arms around my waist and lifting me, breathing me in as my arms clung to his neck.

"Ah, jeez... here we go." Bernardo moaned, rolling his eyes at the sight of me and my superman. Laughing as he tugged his somewhat torn trousers back on (which he had lost when he shifted), he headed off inside the house to check on Carlos.

"I'm sorry I was late, princess." Amadore whispered in my ear, it was going to take him a while to forgive himself, I could tell.

"You looked like you were... dead." I struggled with the words as images of him lying on my floor, drenched in blood haunted me.

"I underestimated him... and he caught me somewhat off guard." he explained, his eyes still hurt, pained at not being able to protect me.

"I never lost faith... ever. You promised me you would never leave me... I knew you wouldn't. I knew it... I love you, Amadore." the last words fell out of my mouth, like my head was afraid to say it but my heart forced them out. The utter delight and joy that spread across his face in that moment was spellbinding, I would say it a million times to see that face, over and over. "Am I a shape shifter?" I asked randomly, making him laugh.

"No, princess. You carry the gene but you're all human... a badass human who's an excellent shot may I add. Unless you have forgotten to tell me that you shift into a little bunny rabbit sometimes?"

"Why a bunny?" I answered back "I'd be something hardcore, like a giant cat or something."

"Like a jaguar?"

"Yes, exactly that."

****

"Did he... touch you?" Amadore's voice was pained and hurt. He was still struggling to look at me, instead keeping his eyes fixed on the road as he drove carefully. I snuggled in the passenger seat, covered with three blankets with the heating on full. Yet, I still felt cold. I had dared a look at my face in the wing mirror of the car and understood why Amadore wasn't looking at me. Just a moment seeing my reflection and I didn't want to either. There was a cut on the bridge of my nose and my left eye could hardly open through the swelling.

"Just my face... with his fist..." Amadore winced at my words and I instantly felt bad about not sugar coating it for him.

"Baby, I'm…"

"Never apologize to me, Amadore…" I interrupted, repeating his words to me "This was not your fault…"

"Yes, it was. I let my guard down at the wrong moment…" he seemed so anguished and tormented, it broke me just witnessing it.

"Did you know he was a shifter?"

"I didn't know until the last moment…" his eyes still stayed locked on the road, my face must really look bad.

"How did you find out? Was it me? Did you sense me?"

"No…" he thought for a moment "I felt drawn to you… but not in a shifter way… you just… shone to me." he dared a peek at me, his hand leaving the gear stick to touch my face, his thumb stroking my cheek "It was your mother, Kate. When I tried to use my mind control on her. Her mind was so clouded. She had no idea why she was there. She spoke the only answer she knew yet…" he thought again "I tried to look closer, to see if she was telling me the truth, but it was so fucked up in her head. I knew she'd been glamoured for years, decades almost."

"So how did you guess my dad?"

"I didn't guess, I asked Bernardo to do some research..." he seemed to drift off into thought

"Tell me what you're thinking...." I asked, placing my hand on his leg, needing him to forgive himself. Needing him to smile so my world would brighten.

"We were in your bedroom... your heart beat was so loud... beating for me. I only just heard Bernardo yelling," he gripped my hand which was still clung to his knee and offered me a smile. A halfhearted, painful smile.

"What was he yelling?"

"That my suspicion was right. That your dad was an old and powerful shifter... and he is on his way... I'd sensed him to, I was just too... preoccupied to care." this whole conversation could wait. It was killing him explaining his failures to me. And it was killing me seeing him in such agonizing pain.

"I dreamt of you...." I offered, earning myself a small grin.

"When...?"

"In the basement..."

"You slept down there?" His face seemed

confused.

"Erm... not through my own choice." My words made him wince again so I quickly continued "But you were there... you were making love to me and I asked you to kill my dad..."

"Bit of a mood killer," he joked, genuine amusement playing behind his eyes, I laughed loudly, needing the release.

"Yeah, anyway... but you said you already had killed him. You told me you had torn his head off." Amadore's eyes shot towards me, staring deep into mine "...Erm, watch the road..." he grinned at me and looked away "That's when I knew you were coming for me, and I knew tonight would end like it did, because even in my dreams, you never break a promise."

"I see... well I'm glad that even when I'm screwing up I can still manage to please you somehow," he grinned, but it still held his pain, torture I knew no words were able to take away right now. I wanted to, with every ounce of me. I would feel everything for him, just so he could feel nothing but happiness.

"You always please me, Superman... yet I doubt you'll want to be doing any pleasing with the state of my face at the minute." I joked, grinning through the pain.

"You kidding me? You look bad-ass," he laughed and pulled my hand upwards, placing it on his face as he smiled at me "I'd make love to you right now if it wasn't incredibly inappropriate."

Chapter 16

"Merry Christmas, princess." Amadore whispered into my ear as I stretched out in his new king-size luxury four-poster bed, the white silk sheets cold on my skin yet the warmth of his naked body heating me from the inside. I shuffled next to him and buried my face in his sweet scented neck.

"Merry Christmas, superman." I replied, sensing his smile as he breathed me in, his hands running up and down my spine, bringing me to wakefulness with hot lust and passion, I couldn't think of a better way to start the day "What's everyone doing?"

"Bernardo and Carlos have gone out briefly to pick up a turkey and deliver some presents, your mother is still asleep." His grin told me what I actually wanted to know, we were alone. My hands slid up into his hair, pulling him down to kiss me, stealing what I needed, what my body ached for. He obliged instantly, sliding his tongue into my mouth and groaning with pleasure as he rolled on top of me and parted my legs with his. His touch electrified me, sparked me to life. Every small movement, every silent noise set fire to my soul, his kisses moved down to my neck as his skilled hands moved between my legs, pushing me forward, upwards.

"Amadore..." I groaned as his kisses continued their journey south around my belly button and downwards still. I knew my heartbeat must have been almost deafening for him, but I had lost all control. I slid my hands into his soft, silky hair as he placed a final kiss on my inner thigh before sliding his skilled tongue over my sex. I drew in a sharp breath and arched my back instinctively, unable to control anything. He had completely overcome me, I was his. His tongue and kisses worked their magic between my legs as I began to quiver. He was so skilled with me, like he was linked to me somehow. Like he knew exactly what to do to make me react this way.

He softened his kisses and began kissing upwards, stopping at my breasts to take them in his mouth, offering them a gentle pinch with his teeth, opening all my nerve endings. I moaned with luscious delight and wrapped my legs around his waist, pulling him towards me, needing him inside me. Slowly, gently, he entered me as his mouth claimed mine, silencing our groans. His steady, soft thrusts brought me higher and higher. I tightened my legs around his waist forcing him deeper, needing more of him, needing all of him.

"I love you, Amadore." I whispered, as he deepened inside me, my words sparking something in him, losing his control with me, taking me as I arched my back, enjoying the best Christmas present I had ever received.

"I love you too, Princess." he whispered in return as my senses heightened and I felt myself build up, a release so close and so needed, he took my breast in his hand and thrust once more, tipping me over the edge as I moaned loudly. He joined me quickly, finding his undoing then kissing me passionately and flopping on top of me all hot, sweaty, sexy as fuck. "Best Christmas present. Ever." He swooned, still a little breathless and still running his hands over my sensitive body, making me quiver beneath him.

"You stole my line." I breathed back, running my hands up and down his back, wishing that I could stay this way all day.

"Your mother is waking up, I think." his eyes glanced briefly towards the door as he concentrated, listening to the sounds coming from her room, two doors down from ours. It had been almost two weeks since Bill...left. Mum quickly broke up with her rich husband, telling me she didn't really think she knew him, and that she wasn't even in love with him. I had my suspicions that Bill perhaps told her to re-marry to a filthy rich man while he was in prison, it would explain how they had a nice cottage just days after his release. But I suppose I'll never know.

  She had been so confused lately, always thinking, like she was trying to remember where her whole life had gone. Bernardo had kindly offered her one of their seven spare bedrooms while she house hunted for a place near me, a fresh start. The past week I had spent more time talking to her than I had my whole life, learning things about her, and she about me. I was surprised to learn that she still knew little things, like how I had my tea and my favorite cartoon as a child. She would often laugh and speak about funny memories from her past, things that actually never happened. I would always laugh along with her, as would the boys. I felt terrible at times, wondering if letting her live a lie was the kindest thing to do, or if I should have given her a chance to get over what she had witnessed. Amadore often assured me that we did the right thing, that she would have never forgiven herself. He was right, but it was still hard to live with at times.

    Amadore kissed my forehead and hopped out of bed, I drank in his view, gloriously naked and utterly divine, he walked over to the master bathroom, sending me a little wink as he disappeared. I jumped out of bed quickly too, and walked to follow him. He was already in the shower as I entered, taking a moment to stare in the mirror, the bruises I had acquired under my left eye from Bill were healing quick and just small yellow smudges now, my hair was messy and my body still throbbing and sensitive.

    "There's room for two, Princess." Amadore called out, opening the shower door and welcoming me inside.

***

    "Oh, Anabelle. You look beautiful!!" my mother swooned, clapping her hands with excitement as she perched up the breakfast bar with a glass of champagne (at ten in the morning) dressed in a cream silk robe, looking more like the queen of the castle than I did. I gave her a spin, letting her see the full effect of my red, backless dress, the diamante straps glistening and ruffles adding extra curves, made more special by the fact that my Amadore picked and bought it for me. The same Amadore that was now gliding smoothly around the giant kitchen, preparing what looked to be a Christmas feast, fit for a king...three kings in fact. Mum poured another glass and handed it to me as I joined her, leaning on the counter, enjoying the view of my superman cooking, dressed smartly in black suit trousers, a crisp white fitted shirt with cufflinks, and a black Armani belt. Noticing me licking my lips, he headed over to join us, sending me a wink as he strolled over, Mum quickly poured a third glass of champagne.

"Thank you, Kate." Amadore offered, taking the glass with one hand and placing the other on my face, caressing my cheek with his thumb "So beautiful," he whispered, leaning in to my ear, nibbling on my ear lobe quickly before standing and pulling me towards him. I wrapped my arms around his waist and tried to remember a Christmas as good as this, knowing full well there wasn't one. The smells of Amadore stood so close, and food he was cooking was heavenly, giant silver saucepans, filled with vegetables bubbled on the old fashion stove, chopping boards placed on the other end of the counter displayed all different sorts of cheeses, a wine rack (that was almost as tall as me) was full with all different sorts of red and white wines and the slow cooker steamed away, cooking what looked to be a huge beef joint.

"Sorry we're late," Carlos yelled, bounding through the giant entrance hall and entering the kitchen "Merry Christmas, Belle." he continued, pushing Amadore out the way, and lifting me in a bear hug, spinning me round as a laugh escaped me. He was always so playful and happy, and he made the whole room that way, radiating everything he felt. He placed me back down on my feet as Amadore's arm appeared back round my waist, he was smiling proudly, happy to watch me so accepted. I was happy, too. I had never felt so safe, so loved. At times, it was hard to digest. I was still so confused as to why I deserved all this. I liked to believe it was God's plan for me all along, that I had to survive a cruel childhood, to get to live the dream here, with Amadore. I knew that there possibly wouldn't be anything I wouldn't endure, just to be here, next to him.

Amadore kissed my forehead and pulled

out a bar stool, offering me a seat and helping me hop up as he headed back to finish his cooking. I took a sip of my champagne, letting the bubbles pop in my mouth for a moment before swallowing it.

"Merry Christmas, Anabelle," Bernardo's voice growled as he bent towards me, he had never once come near me, and now he was about to kiss my cheek. I felt the old me sneaking through and felt the start of panic settling in my stomach. *He is no threat; he is no threat.* My conscience scolded as my eyes met with Amadore's. He was watching carefully, knowing my fears. He reacted the exact same way when Carlos hugged me for the first time one week ago. I managed to stay calm then... I breathed in and focused. Smiling at my superman quickly, I turned back to Bernardo and wrapped one arm around him and kissed his cheek back in return.

"Merry Christmas to you, too." I grinned as he pulled away and patted my head and headed over to the kitchen area to offer his help. Amadore was smiling fondly when my eyes met with his again. I grinned back as he laughed, seemingly proud of me. To be honest, I was sort of proud of myself too.

"Well, I'm going to get dressed as I'm the only one not looking like a million pounds," Mum interrupted as Carlos grinned.

"Personally, I disagree Mrs. Jones. I think you look textbook-perfect." His eyes darkened as he grinned. *cringe*.

"Oh, Carlos. You are a cutie." my mum touched his shoulder briefly before hopping off her stool and sweeping off upstairs to change.

"*Me... and... Mrs.... Mrs. Jones!*" Carlos sang as Bernardo erupted with laughter and my face fell into my hands to hide the fact I found it kind of funny also. Carlos was over twenty years my mum's junior. Still, he loved women and just couldn't help himself. There was a small part of me that hoped my mum had the sense to not go there.

"Behave yourself and do the stuffing for this turkey, would you?" Amadore ordered, amusement ringing behind his voice as he pretended to not find it funny too, for my sake I guessed.

"Oh! I'll be stuffing something, alright!" Carlos joked as we all burst out laughing - that side splitting, mascara ruining, jaw aching laugh.

****

Bernardo had lit a fire in the huge fireplace in the lounge and even though the room itself was massive, with tall ceilings and mammoth windows it heated it up nicely, making it homely and inviting. We were all full to the brim with deliciously food the boys had cooked up. I had imagined that any normal day they would have flew around the kitchen a lot faster than they did, but considering my mum was watching most of the time, they acted like normal, fun loving, playful brothers. Not the shape shifting gods I knew they were.

We all settled down, Amadore and I snuggled on the couch together, stretching out our legs as he whispered sweet words in my ears, and occasionally making sarcastic comments about his brothers or making dirty innuendos at things Carlos said to my mum. Bernardo and Carlos lounged on the fur rug in front of the fire and mum sunk into the arm chair, curling her legs up and smiling contently at the three brothers, joking and laughing with each other. As Bernardo and Carlos got into a heated debate about a television programme they were both into, my mother joining in, I took the opportunity to hand Amadore his Christmas present I had made him. It took me ages to decide what to do. I mean, what do you buy a man that has everything?

"I thought we decided you weren't buying anything? you've already given me everything I could ever want." Amadore said, but with a hint of excitement behind his eyes.

"Yes, we did decide that, that's why I didn't buy you anything... I made you something." I replied, feeling smug I found the loop hole in his deal.

"I see," he breathed, taking the present wrapped in gold paper with a small silver bow "Even more special then."

"Don't get your hopes up, it's not very good." I grimaced, hoping he wasn't expecting something amazing. I loved being creative, that didn't mean I was good at it though. He shuffled up and pulled me closer, keeping one arm around me, he pulled at the paper as his bracelet fell out. He held it close and examined the blue, yellow and red thread, plaited and woven together simply. A smile swept over his face, I was unsure if he was confused about my choice of colors.

"It's the colors of..."

"Superman." he interrupted, making me breath in a deep breath.

"I made it for you... because..."

"I'm *your superman*." he finished my sentence again as I blushed. Feeling childish and foolish, I hid my eyes under my lashes "There is nothing more perfect than this, princess. Tie it on my wrist for me." he handed me the bracelet and began undoing his cufflink.

"You don't have to wear it," I offered, still feeling a little silly.

"I want to wear it; in fact- I'll never take it off." His words were honest and his smile genuine, leaving my butterflies fluttering and my smug smile reappearing back on my face. I tied it on his wrist as he pulled my face to his, His lips kissing mine so passionately and intensely. I had almost forgotten that we had company as I slid my tongue into his mouth and heard my mum cough, interrupting me.

"Oh... sorry." I blushed as she laughed.

"More champagne?" she asked, tilting the bottle my way.

"We'll be back for champagne in a moment, Kate. But first I need to give Anabelle her present." Amadore said as he rose to his feet and held out his hand to me.

"You'll give her something alright! A good ole' sweaty sh-"

"CARLOS!" me, Bernardo and Amadore yelled in sync, making him burst out laughing.

"Please, excuse my brother, Kate." Amadore offered as he placed his hand on the small of my back and lead me out of the room.

"Where are we going?" I asked as we left the room.

"To the bedroom for a 'good ole' sweaty' shag." Amadore whispered as I heard Bernardo and Carlos explode with laughter, Superman sent me a wink, assuring me he was joking, although I wasn't too sure I wanted him to be. "I noticed the other day at your apartment, you have a driving license," he continued "Why don't you have a car?" he asked as I stopped walking and looked at him.

"Because I can't afford to run one, Amadore please tell me you haven't -" he interrupted me again as he took my hand and dragged me to the front door.

"Please, Anabelle. Just accept my gift and be happy with me. Your present to me was priceless and I loved it and accepted it instantly. Please give me the same treatment." He kissed my forehead then opened the door.

I was faced with the most breath taking car I have ever seen in my life, black and white and sexy as hell "An Audi r8. For you, Princess." he whispered as I stuttered, instantly wanting to tell him that I couldn't accept it, and there was no way I could afford to run it either, but his eyes were staring at me, delightful and excited and in desperate need of approval "Tax and insurance is all paid up for as long as you want it, I'll fill up the tank whenever it gets low too. Unless you don't like it, then we'll take it back and get something you do."

"Amadore..." I was so torn, I didn't deserve this, I couldn't accept this, but I needed to make him happy. "I made you a fucking bracelet, for Christ sake." I choked on a laugh, the whole situation seemed absurd.

"Your bracelet could buy a million of these in my eyes." he shot back, I knew I wasn't winning this.

"I have only known you for six weeks." I tried again.

"But we will be together forever." his eyes softened as he realized his present might be rejected. "Tell me you like it, please."

"Superman... I don't like it... I love it." I gave

in as he grabbed me and spun me round, laughing loudly and kissing my face and neck "Let's take this bad boy for a spin!" I added.

"Oh, hell no. its icy…and you've been drinking." I glared at him as I headed down the steps and over to the sexiest car I had ever seen.

"Oh, please!" I begged as his face suddenly looked dead serious and his eyes stared out down the driveway. I turned my head to see what he was looking at, but nothing was there. "What's the matter?" I asked as I turned back to face him. His expression was once again completely normal.

"Nothing, princess. Now come inside… its cold out here." he said as he took my hand pulling me inside and into his embrace before kicking the door closed behind us.

*****

Amadore strolled up to the bed where I laid, he was wearing nothing but a blue, yellow and red bracelet and a smoldering grin, I pulled the white silk covers back as he climbed in and slid over to me, covering himself up before wrapping his toned, muscular arms around me and planting a kiss on my lips. He had seemed nothing but completely normal since we were outside, I was beginning to think I was the crazy one, perhaps it was me seeing things, not him.

"Thank you for my present." I said again, although it was about the tenth time tonight I had said it.

"Anything for you, Princess. You deserve the absolute best." he replied as I snuggled closer to him, his warmth heating me to my core.

"So do you though."

"I have the best, I have you." I thought for a while, amazed at him and the words he chooses. How does he make a girl who has so little to offer, feel so special? I had something to live for now. My prayers had been answered.

"You said earlier that we will be together forever?" I asked, needing to hear it again.

"Yes, Princess. I did. And I meant it... you and me were written in the stars."

Chapter 17

My feet sunk into the cold wet mud as I looked around. Trees surrounded me as far as I could see, the chilling fog coated the ground. I listened quietly as animal noises got louder and louder. Growls and hoots made me begin to run, afraid. They were after me; I knew that much. Twigs snapped under my feet, stones and rocks tore at my skin. But I couldn't stop running. I lost my footing as I tripped, the coldness slapping me in the face as mud splashed into my eyes and hair. *He didn't catch me...he always catches me* my subconscious thought, pain etching through the fear.

"RUN, ANABELLE!" I heard my superman order as I scrambled to my feet, wet and cold, frightened and alone. My feet were heavy as I powered forward, pushing past branches as they whipped my face and tangled in my long hair, but I didn't stop. I kept running, I was in grave danger. I knew that for sure. The temperature dropped dramatically as I entered a snow covered field, lit up by the moon. This wasn't the way. There is nowhere to hide. I must run, he told me to run.

I felt his arms surround me before I even

knew he was there, then everything shot past me, I couldn't see, couldn't breathe. Yet I knew I was safe in his arms, he had me now. He was running with me. Then everything stopped and I was placed on to my feet. Fear was still injected into me as I glanced back towards the forest. Men and animals fought savagely and loudly. I squinted to see Carlos and Bernardo... losing. Blood covered. Dead. My breath escaped me as my mouth opened to scream. Nothing came out. I took one step forward, I had to help, even if I died trying. It was then I noticed Amadore being torn from the field, scrapping fiercely with two men and a grey wolf, he was still alive, just. It was then I realized the presence I felt behind me, wasn't my superman.

    I turned my head slightly as my conscience screamed at me to run, yet - if the Renato brothers were to die tonight, then I wished to also. I wished with everything inside me that this man behind me would kill me too.

    "Anabelle..." his voice snarled as I turned to see him, he dressed all in black and radiated power, his long black hair fell all the way down his back, shining and deadly straight. His face was old and slightly wrinkled and his eyes were black. I stared into them, wanting them to read my soul, wondering if I was to punch him square in the jaw it would make this go quicker, the fighting behind me had died down, the sounds had gone quiet. Bile rose in my throat as I wondered why, perhaps Amadore had already lost, already dead.

"Who are you?" I asked, unsure why. His snow white skin wrinkled more as he grinned.

"You need to know who you are first, Anabelle."

"I know who I am." I answered as a breezed drifted past me onto him. He breathed in my scent like it made his mouth water, his hands instinctively clasped my face, his strength was undeniable.

"*What* you are, Anabelle." he barked as I yanked myself backwards, freeing myself from his grip.

"Don't touch me!" I ordered as he lunged forward, knocking me to the cold icy ground and pinning me to the floor "STOP IT!! GET OFF!!" I yelled, hitting and punching out.

"ANABELLE, STOP IT!" His mouth moved, yet this time his voice was different...recognizable "ANABELLE!" tears streamed down my face as the cold snow turned to silk. I blinked through the blur as the stranger's face turned into the man I loved and my surroundings become clear.

    I jumped out of bed, in desperate need to feel awake, needing to believe what I was seeing was real, not a dream.

    "Bernardo and Carlos?" I demanded at Amadore, as he sat in bed, his eyes wild with fear and confusion, his hand reaching out for me.

    "Are behind the door." he informed me as I walked to the end of the bed and retrieved my night gown and threw it on before running to the door to open it. There they stood. No cuts. No blood. Alive. Tears still ran down my face as the image of them dead haunted me more. I watched them make eye contact with Amadore. They were so beautiful alive. All three of them glowed with strength and power. With life. "What's going on, Princess?" Amadore questioned, panic shaking through his beautiful voice.

    "A dream…" my legs began to shake as the stranger's face scorched my memory. My feet wobbled wearily back over to the bed as Amadore caught me, pulling me into his embrace. "A terrible dream."

    "What happened?" he asked as Bernardo and Carlos entered the room and crouched next to me, waiting patiently for me to talk.

"You all... died," I began to feel silly, it was - after all - just a dream. Wasn't it? "Saving me..." I continued as I looked towards Amadore. His gorgeous eyes displayed sympathy as he appeared to look deep into my soul.

"It was just a dream, Princess... Look... We're all still here." His words were warm and welcoming to my ears. I glanced at all three brothers in turn, admiring each one's beauty and charm... a smile crept on to my face as I realized that there was just three men here in this room... yet a whole army could not stand against them. They were heroes, warriors... and I was dumb for even thinking that they could be harmed.

"Sorry..." I muttered, suddenly feeling unworthy of the support they were giving me.

"Don't apologies..." Carlos offered "Want me to fetch you a drink? Water? Coffee?" I sent him a half grin, wanting to say more but not having the words.

"No, it's okay. Thank you" he nodded to my response and rose to his feet as Bernardo followed.

"Thanks guys." Amadore added as they left the room. I looked at my superman. So beautiful and spectacular. I should have known. It was just a dream, yet, even if it wasn't, the idea that he would die protecting me didn't seem that absurd. In fact, the look in his eyes told me that he would happily lose his life to guard mine.

I hated that thought.

I ran my fingers through my hair, feeling angry; yet I was unsure why. The dream had affected me more than I cared to admit. The face of the stranger seemed to have scorched the insides of my eyelids. I didn't dare close my eyes; I didn't want to ever see his face again...

"Talk to me, princess." Amadore whispered. his face seemed concerned and his brows were knitted tightly together, beautiful frown lines decorated his face. I reached up and allowed my finger to trace them, to smooth them out.

"Distract me... Talk to me." I bit down on my lip as he thought for a moment then smiled. Leaning forward he undid my dressing gown slowly and I let it slip from my shoulders. Gently, he stood me up and threw the silk gown across the room and lifted the bed sheets.

"I had a dream too..." he whispered as he lifted my naked body into his arms and kissed my forehead before lying me between the sheets and covering me over. "A good dream…" I grinned as he made his way around to the other side of the bed. I felt my nightmare slipping from me as he continued to speak, his glorious body shining like a Gods in the moonlight. "I built you a home… but… we had no electric." he went on as a grin so overwhelmingly astonishing claimed his face, like his was recalling the whole dream I was now too desperate to hear about.

"Oh… What did we do…?" I asked as he slipped into bed and shuffled close to me.

"I found that… when you smiled at me… I could see everything clearly. It was never dark for me… not when we were together." My heart ached and any last memory of my nightmare vanished. I watched him wet his lips before he continued, realizing I was utterly spellbound and hooked on his every word. "We had a picket fence… white, of course. Hard wood floors. Pretty yellow flowers in pots on the kitchen window sill." He paused for a moment to look at me, I laughed and shook my head, trying to shake away the trance I felt had a hold on me.

Suddenly he looked towards the door and appeared to be listening to something that I couldn't hear...

"What is it?" I asked as he continued to listen for a moment or two.

"I've got to go out for a while. Will you be OK?" he asked as I sat up and clutched the sheets to my chest.

"Where? Why?" it was just gone two in the morning and, to be honest, I didn't want to be alone.

"A job. I won't be long, princess. Promise. I'll be home before you wake up."

"What sort of job? Can I come?" I asked, hoping I could just go along for the ride, perhaps wait in the car or something.

"Absolutely not." he was already out of bed and throwing on his clothes. Even fully dressed he was a picture of perfection. Grabbing his duffel coat off the back of the chair he made his way back over to me, fastening it to the top before bending down to kiss my forehead. "Go to sleep, princess." I already felt empty and he hadn't even left the room yet. The idea that he was about to run out of this house into danger frightened me more than I thought it would. I really still didn't have a clue about his job. he had never spoken about it and often changed the conversation when I tried to. However, I knew it was dangerous. That was perhaps the one thing I would wish not to know. I wondered briefly who had hired him this time, and why it was so sudden and urgent. My eyes must have given me away because he sat down on the edge of the bed and took my face in his hands. "Baby, if I let you come with me... I will be completely incapable of doing the job I need to. When you are near me... you claim all my attention without even trying. I need to be focused... and you need to be safe." I winced as anxiety trickled into me. I wanted to ask what he needed to be focused on, but the most part of me didn't want to know. It would only make me feel worse.

"Promise you'll be here in the morning...?" I asked as he thought for a moment and it made my stomach twist into a painful knot. What was there to think about? was there a chance he wouldn't be?

"I promise." he finally said and drew me into a long kiss. before disappearing out of the door in a blink.

I opened the bedside drawer and grabbed his phone and headphones. Shuffling into to sheets I powered up his BlackBerry and selected his 'favorites' play list. I went to sleep as his favorite band sung in my ears... something about true love. At one point they sang 'the little that I have to give, I'll give it all to you.'

That made me smile.

****

I rubbed my eyes and quickly sat up and glanced at the clock. It was just before eight am, and I was alone. I told myself not to panic, to remain calm, but my feet had a mind of their own as they jumped out of bed. I quickly opened Amadore's wardrobe and stole a shirt to throw on before exiting the bedroom and running down the hall.

"Amadore...?" I said, quiet enough to not wake mum, but loud enough so he would hear... nothing. I took the giant stairs downwards as fast as I could I wandered through into the kitchen. Everywhere seemed too quiet. Too lonely.

I began to pace, deciding what to do. Go get changed... get in my fast car... go find him... *how'd ya plan on doing that, smartass?* my conscience scorned, making me think of plan b... then c... and so on. I must have been panicking for longer than I thought as I heard the front door slam and the voices of three Gods talking quietly to each other.

"Amadore…" I let out a breath as I bounded into his arms.

"What's the matter?" he asked urgently.

"You are, I was worried!" I stated as I pulled backwards to look at him, noticing blood in his hair and on his forehead. "What happened? Are you alright?" I could sense Bernardo and Carlos watching, but I didn't care. Amadore pulled my hand away from his head and smiled at me nervously.

"It's… not my blood, princess." He replied as I finally looked around. All three brothers were dirty and bloodied, their clothes ripped and distressed.

"Is any of it any of yours…?" I whispered quietly as they looked at each other, deciding who should answer.

"I cut my fist punching someone's face…" Carlos stated, making Amadore shake his head exasperated. I had no idea where they had been, what they had done, who they had hurt or what they had earned doing it. This was the biggest secret of all. Not that they have these powers, it's what they do with them. That's what frightened me the most.

"Okay... as long as you're all fine." I offered, turning on my heels and heading upstairs to shower. I wanted to be angry at them, but it wasn't my place. I had walked into their lives, not them into mine. They owed me no answers. I just worried. They are all I have... my Amadore is all I have. I could never lose him.

I wandered back into the bedroom and headed straight for the shower. Stripping off and hoping in, I allowed the hot water to rinse away all my worry. I think that I will always be this way, everyday wondering if today is the day I'll lose him, the day he leaves.

"Princess...?" Amadore's voice sounded from outside the shower "Can I join you?" I grinned at his request. It could not have been a more welcome one if he tried. Well maybe 'can I join you? I have cake?' might have worked just as well. I made a point of opening the shower door wide, giving him the full effect of my wet, naked body as I smiled darkly at him.

"You said that you'd be home before I woke up." I tried to sound sad, angry at him, instead I just sounded horny as hell. He grinned.

"Yes, I did. Tut, tut. What will you do with me...?" he pulled his torn, dusty shirt off and threw it to one side and began undoing his belt buckle.

"Get in here, naughty man... and be quiet about it."

****

The field I was stood in was beautiful. Daisies in all different colors blew in the warm breeze and tickled the bottom of my bare feet. I smiled to myself as the sun peeked over the horizon, warming my skin to the core. I vaguely wondered how it was this warm in December, but I didn't care. It was a dream. I knew that much.

My white silk and lace dress blew casually in the wind as I looked down and laughed.

"Hi, princess." Amadore swooned as his hands appeared around my waist and embraced me firmly. I smiled to myself as I turned to meet his gaze. He was dressed in just white linen trousers, his gorgeous auburn hair a perfect frame for his face. In the bright sunshine of my dream he looked even more perfect than I had ever seen, and more angelic than Gabriel himself. "What are you doing here?" he asked.

"Dreaming, I believe." I grinned back as my hands instinctively ran over his hard torso, sparking all my senses to life.

"Dreaming in my dream, are you?" he laughed as he took my hand and began to slowly walk with me through the field. "I imagine beautiful images like this all the time. Yet, recently they just don't have the same effect... not unless you're in it." he smiled. "I used to think I could be anything I wanted... now... I can't. I can't be anything... except be in love with you..." his words were making my skin heat up warmer than the sun's rays, yet I felt confused...

Who's dream was this? Was it his? Or mine?

"Amadore... are you sleeping?" I asked as he looked down at me and bit his bottom lip. Raising his thumb to stroke my cheek gently he sighed. "you tell me, Princess... you're the one invading my dream." He laughed and went to walk forward again but I held him back.

"No, this is my dream." I answered, still confused, but he just laughed and wrapped his arms around me.

"Oh, is it? My apologies, princess." Kissing my forehead tenderly he took my gaze

"Well, if that's the case. How can I tell you secrets? For example…" he thought for a moment and grinned "I knew you'd be mine from the moment I saw you… I watched you… memorized by you. The time in the shop wasn't a coincidence either. I'd do anything for you, be whoever you want… whatever you need."

The edges of my dream began to fade and drift as I slowly came back. His glowing face was the last thing I saw. He smiled and lit the way back home. Back to him. I stretched out with a grin and blinked my eyes open, my hands searching the bed for Amadore's warmth and my insides rejoicing when they found him. I lifted my weight onto one arm as I rolled over to look at him, only to have my breath snatched away.

He was asleep.

The sight made my heart hurt. I had never seen him asleep before because, as he once told me, he needs very little. Yet, he was sleeping now. And he looked so magnificent.

One arm was rested under his head as the other lay by his side. His face held no expression, apart from the occasional smile which twitched at the sides of his perfectly shaped lips. The way his eyelashes fanned over his cheeks was so stunning it made me want to reach out and touch them, but I was too afraid to wake him. Afraid of this moment ending, afraid it will be all too long before I get to witness this again.

Then it hit me.

Who's dream was it?

It was definitely mine. I dreamt it. I remembered it... right?

"Everything OK, princess?" Amadore asked as he woke to see me staring off, deep in thought.

"You were asleep...?" I asked, needing to make sure before I asked a question which was undoubtedly going to make me sound crazy.

"Yes... what's the matter?" he questioned again, this time sitting up to look at me and placing his hand on my face.

"Did you have a dream?" I asked as the color literally drained from him. "You did... didn't you?" I questioned again as his head began to nod and his hand dropped from my cheek.

"Bernardo!" Amadore yelled making me jump as he shot out of bed and tugged on some sweat pants and stood, frozen. Staring at me.

Bernardo and Carlos burst in and stood beside him, making me grab the sheets and hold them tight around my chest, thankful for my long hair that was covering my back. All three brothers staring at me made me feel uneasy, and perhaps a little scared.

"Amadore... what's happening?" I asked, tears pricking in my eyes.

"It's OK, just..." he thought for a second as he ran his fingers through his hair, fear and desperation were injected into his eyes and I knew this was bad. Really bad. "I should have seen this long before now..." he continued, this time directing his words to his brothers as I shuffled backwards in the bed. "When she was captured she dreamt of me... and I told her we had already killed her dad... but at the time, we hadn't." Carlos grinned at me and placed his hands on his hips as Amadore and Bernardo shared worried glances with each other.

"Could it be just a coincidence?" Bernardo's voice growled as I bit my lip and drew my legs up to my chest.

"I hoped..." Amadore replied as he walked cautiously up the bed and offered me a sympathetic grin as he sat down next to me and wrapped his arm around my shoulders. "It's ok, baby. Don't be scared." he whispered into my hair as he looked towards his brothers. "She just... she was in my dream. Like... actually."

Bernardo sucked in a deep breath as Carlos nodded in what looked like acceptance... maybe appreciation, I wasn't sure. Amadore held me tighter as I looked up into his eyes.

"What have I done wrong...?" I asked.

"Nothing princess... nothing you couldn't help."

"What's going on then?" I looked at all three brothers in turn, all reluctant to keep me in the loop. Although, I knew the one who would.

"Amadore. Tell me."

"You're a Dream Watcher, princess."

The secrets he kept.

Peek-a-boo, mother fucker I thought as I spotted him. Me and my Brothers had sensed a shifter in our area for around three days, never quite able to spot him or stalk him down, until now. I knew who he was as soon as I spotted him, I knew he was corrupt. He had escaped from a secret secure unit a week ago and all shifters had received letters about him, we were to capture and return him, dead or alive.

I was unsure why he was sentenced to spend his life time in a S.S.U but watching him eye up a pretty, young lady as she walked beneath me I got a rough idea. I knew I had to intervene. I swooped down, getting a thrill from the wind rippling through the feathers of my wings, which stretched out as I plunged towards the ground and landed on the snow covered wall as the young prey walked past. My brothers would kill me for taking him on alone, but what else could I do? Let him hurt the girl? The innocent... stunningly beautiful, dangerously alluring girl...?

I froze as she walked up to me, turning my insides to ash. *Who is she...?* I thought as she smiled, I was shifted... I was a crow. Why is she looking at me like that? More importantly, why was she just stood there...? *Do something, idiot!* my sub-conscious scorned at me.

"A little creepy, don't ya think, Mr. Crow?" she said as her laugh floated through the air, so heavenly. But he was gaining on her, and in this moment I knew, without any doubt, I was not going to allow one hair on her precious, magnificent head be harmed tonight. Or ever.

I squawked loudly, hoping to frighten her, she had to run. He was gaining on her, and my suspicions told me he wasn't after a friendly conversation. I watched intently as she peered round, spotting her stalker, fear injected into her eyes instantly. She was anxious about strangers?

I took off into the sky, aware I had to get back to my car, grab my clothes and be back to her, all in about thirty seconds. A challenge I knew I could complete in twenty. My wings stretched and soared into the air, gliding me with speed towards my Jag. A quick glance around told me no one could see me as I came in to land in the deserted cul-de-sac I was parked in. I shifted back in the air. I felt myself slide into my human form. That brief moment in between forms was like being set free, like stretching out after twelve hours' sleep. I felt my skin become smooth, and saw sparks as black feathers disintegrated into the night. I was human seconds before I hit the ground, landing safely on my bare feet.

I moved as fast as I physically could, which was fast (around two hundred and ninety miles an hour) I popped my boot and grabbed my clothes, throwing them on as I darted back towards the direction she was heading. I was almost there as I slid on my last boot mid stride and threw my coat on. As I drew nearer to her I heard sobs as her footsteps beat quickly and hard on the ground. She was running. I shot out of a dark alley and saw her, pounding towards me. He was behind her, enjoying the chase. Getting a thrill from her crying, running.

"Stop..." I whispered, knowing she wouldn't hear me, but he would. And he did. He glared at me with menacing promises to seek revenge and a part of me welcomed it, I was excited to rip him apart for frightening this wonderfully enchanting girl... who was about to fall on her face. *Shit.*

I shot forward, taking the four-meter distance in milliseconds and caught her as my hopes rose into my throat. *Look at me, you beautiful creature...* my voice sounded in my head... but she didn't. Her eyes darted behind her, as her stalker turned and left. Her intense fear radiated off her and her stunning body shook through her panic. I wanted to take it all away from her. I had to. There wasn't one part of me that could watch her like this. I imagined how utterly breath-taking she must be when she laughed, or danced. Images of me and her together stole my mind. I wanted to hold her, kiss her, be with her always.

Her head turned to me but her eyes stayed looking down. *Look at me... I'll save you if you look at me...* I bit my lip as I cursed myself. I was acting like a crazy man, but she had me already. Hook, line and sinker - I was hers. My hands stayed locked onto her and she fitted in them perfectly, as her eyes rose to meet mine my breath got caught in my throat. *Fucking hell... she's amazing... say something, you idiot!*

"Are you OK?" *Of course she isn't, you tool!* my face fought to stay mutual, my body fighting not to swoop her up and take her away.

"I... Erm..." her stuttering made my heart melt, so precious. In that instant she broke free and stepped backwards, leaving me cold, empty and completely worthless, like a writer with no words. "Sorry." she whimpered again, destroying me further. Angels like her should never apologize. You only ever say sorry when you're wrong, and she was the opposite of wrong in every single way.

"Don't be." I had to smile at myself, she was stealing my words away and turning me into a speechless weirdo and there wasn't a damn thing I could do about it. I felt sucked in, drawn to her like the eye of a hurricane, I prayed deep inside that she would tear through my entire life. Take everything and throw it in the air, then dance with me underneath it all.

"I... erm... didn't know him." she clarified again, her stutter making me grin at the utterly perfect sound of her voice.

"I see." *for Christ sake, Amadore, ask a question at least!* "Where are you off to at this time of night?" *Well done.*

"Home. I just finished work." Work? Women like her should sit in a castle and be showered with everything and anything they wish, not working.

"Let me walk you there." I replied, I could still sense the shifter between the mist of my craziness, she was still in danger.

"Thank you, but I only live a few minutes away, I should be fine." *but you won't be,* I thought. I knew what I had to do, yet toying with such a delicately beautiful head like hers seemed illegal. *She's just a human... get a grip...*

"More the reason for me to walk you there, it's not out of my way. *Please.*" I sent a touch of control in the last word, hoping that was all I needed, cursing myself for doing it. I watched carefully as her mind swallowed my words, digesting what I had said, was she fighting it?

"OK... Thank you." *Phew.*

"Lead the way." *and when we get there, take me inside and invite me into your bedroom* "My name is Amadore Renato." *probably more appropriate.*

"Erm... I'm Anabelle... Anabelle Jones." I was almost too busy thinking how Anabelle Renato had a much better ring to it to notice her skidding on the ice again. My hands instinctively darted out and caught her again. I felt her aura rush into me like a bus hitting me in the face. The warmness of her skin making me squeeze harder than perhaps I should, the smell of her hair making my mouth water. "Sorry, again." she whispered. I felt something like anger as I thought she said that word much more than she should. Perhaps she's spent her whole life apologizing for something. That thought twisted at my stomach.

We dropped into single file and headed through a dark alley and I couldn't help but feel glad I walked her back home. Mostly because I could feel the shifter still close by, and if he didn't get to her first, she was bound to slip and break her neck.

"It was a pleasure to meet you tonight, Anabelle." I spoke, it came out much more confidently than I felt inside. For that, I was glad. I smiled as her face twisted into a confused and somewhat worried expression as she dug deep into her satchel. She seemed the sort to lose her head if it wasn't attached. Too busy dreaming and talking to birds I bet. "Everything alright?"

"I can't find my…" I bit down hard on my lip to disguise my smile at her delight as she pulled her keys out of her bag. Her face when even slightly happy was mind-blowing. It made me want to laugh out loud. "Bingo." she added as I hid my emotions before she glanced back at me.

"You are very amusing to me, Belle. May I call you that?" I cursed myself for my honest outburst, but deep inside me knew that I couldn't just let her walk inside without any sort of bond. I needed her to remember me. I knew I needed to see her again.

"Yes, you may. However, I don't really see what you're finding amusing." *oh, crap!* I thought. Trying to make a bond and end up pissing her off. I thought quickly, needing to recover.

"Your eyes, you are charming to me." I could have sworn my palms were sweating. Her stunning eyes floated to mine and her face softened. I prayed I'd saved myself.

"Oh..." she stuttered "Thanks." *Great, now she thinks you weird!* I wanted to read her thoughts, to hear what she was thinking.

"Hopefully we will meet again soon." I added as I realized I was staring at her. I tried to soften my glare but had no chance. She had me spellbound.

"Hopefully." she said simply. Leaving me hoping. I could still sense the shifter in the area and realizing I still had a job to do, I decided to push my luck. If she let me walk her to her door, I could at least see where she lives. Then I'll call my brothers and together we can take him out. That way, no harm comes to her.

"Perhaps you wouldn't mind if I walked you

to your door, to make sure you get into your flat safely? *please?*" I sent a touch of control with my last word again, hoping that she would allow me to walk her to her door anyway, but just in case she didn't.

"Erm..." she thought for a moment, her brows furrowing as she decided what to do. I wanted her to trust me. To look into my soul and see I would never cause her harm. Yet, she was mindful and weary of me. In fact, thinking about it, she seemed almost a little frightened of the world. The way she stood, the way she held herself, the way her long dark curls hid her stunning face. It was like she wished to disappear. She hurt. I could almost feel it radiating from her, I had to fix her. "Yes, please do." she added and I couldn't help the smile that invaded my face. Perhaps she did trust me. A little.

"Wonderful. After you, Belle," I took the door from her and held it open. I couldn't work out if she was really confident with me, or whether it was a show. If she even felt slight nerves with me- it never showed. Although her body language said she was quite reserved, it was how her eyes looked into mine. Like she saw into me. Even in my crow form, she looked right into my eyes, like she knew.

We got to the top of the stairs as she slowed and walked over to her door.

"This is my one here. Number seventeen." she added. Just breathing in I could smell the other shifter. He had been here already. He already knew where she lived. How long has he been following her? What did he want with her? *Perhaps what you want, Amadore?* my subconscious replied with sarcasm. I noticed her looking at me as I quickly disguised my concern. She didn't have to know. There was no point worrying her and telling her that she was in danger. After all, she isn't anymore. I would never allow that. She would always be safe now.

"Goodnight, Belle. *Sleep well.*" I added more mind control. If I was to fight and kill another shifter in her home tonight, I didn't want her seeing. She had to sleep through. "*Leave a window open.*" I added. If the shifter came back tonight, he would be able to sense if I had walked through the door. So I wouldn't. I'd fly through the window. I offered her a final grin, one I hoped she would remember, as I headed back down the stairs and outside to call my brothers.

"Feathers?" Bernardo growled. The stupid nick name I had acquired over the years still had its effect. It pissed me off. However, the situation at hand was more important than scolding my older brother.

"Found him." I stated, knowing he would know exactly what I was talking about.

"Where?"

"I'm at the top of Ketts Hill. He's after a girl." *My girl.* "I've followed her back to her home. I'm waiting for him to show his face."

"I'll get Carlos. Be there in five." he hung up. I glanced up towards her flat just as she slid her window open. *Good girl...* I thought to myself as I glanced around. It was late the surrounding houses all looked locked down and all lights off apart from the street lamp glowing dimly above me. Knowing it was about time I broke into her house, I found some coverage behind a bush by the front door and stripped off, leaving my clothes hidden for later.

Then shifted.

Although my speed and strength as a human was phenomenal, my sight as a crow was just something else. I could zoom in and see things miles away as if they were right in front of me which was quite handy when flying as high as I liked to.

I took off up to the window and perched

briefly on the ledge, *The bedroom window, Anabelle? Really?* I thought. Any other window would have done, now I have to attempt to walk past her, while all the time, wanting to shift back and climb into bed with her. After deciding that this was going to be even harder than fighting the shifter I got to work. Swooping quietly into her room I hopped the length of the bedroom in case the flapping of my wings woke her.

"Amadore..." she whispered as I froze. *Crap.*

I peered up at her... but she was asleep.

She's dreaming of me...

It was then that I hopped and landed on her bed frame, watching her sleep. My insides rejoiced as she rolled over, whispering my name. *You're safe now...* I thought, knowing it was true. I could sense my brothers getting close and I knew I had to get to work.

First I would kill this shifter for daring to hurt this girl.

Then I would make this girl mine.

Music kept me writing and helped me feel the emotions when I needed a little help. Here is my track list to 'The secrets I keep'. It's all the songs I played in those long nights, whilst I dreamed this book to life.

1) Dear True Love- Sleeping at Last.
2) I'm Yours- The Script.
3) Little Things- One Direction.
4) Don't You Remember- Adele.
5) First Time Ever I Saw Your Face- Easther Bennett.
6) Romeo and Juliet- Dire Straits.
7) Superman- Sabrina.
8) Clown- Emeli Sande.
9) Change (In The House of Flies)- Deftones.
10) I Need You Now- Olly Murs.
11) Rewind- Paolo Nutini.
12) I'd Come for You- Nickelback.
13) Shadow- Janis Ian.
14) Kissing You- Desree.
15) Addicted- Enrique Iglesias.
16) Wilderness- Sleeping at Last.
17) God Gave Me You- Blake Shelton.

Acknowledgements.

I have to start with thanking my mum, for without you passing down your creative abilities and teaching me to believe in me, I wouldn't have got this far. But as you say mum, it was written in the stars.

To my siblings, Danielle and Jamie. Thank you for protecting me in all my own personal battles, for never losing faith in me and for your constant support. I take your strength and encouragement with me everywhere- 'even if you cannot hear my voice, I'll be right beside you, dear.' 'when you feel like you're done, and the darkness has won... babe, you're not lost.'

Morgan-Leigh, you'll never know how you saved me, and I'll probably never tell you. But, between you and me, you'll always be the reason I'm breathing. Thank you princess, you graced me with your life at just the right time.

My gorgeous boy, Edward. I smile when I see you, because I know my little girls will always be looked after. I cannot wait to see the big, strong boy you will become. you've already made me so proud.

Daddy, your support never goes unnoticed, knowing you have faith in me is my driving force. I love to see you full of pride. 'Any man can be a father, but it takes some very special to be a daddy.'

Pat, thank you for taking the time to read my book and

helping with the proof reading. Your support and encouragement was just what I needed.

Georgia, thank you for always giving me something to do, my life would be so dull without you. I enjoy learning life lessons with you, you teach me new things every day.

Kayleigh, thank you for always being there when I need you. Whether we speak every day or every month, I always know you'll help if I ask you to. I find it easy now to write about friendships that can last lifetimes... I just think about you.

To all my friends and family giving me strength along the way. Demi, Stevie, Fay, Auntie Lu and Dean. My lovely Nanny. My sister-in-law Sam, Sharon, Amanda, Michaela. Your support made me brave. Made this possible.

To my Husband, my own personal superman. For putting up with me through all the hours I spent attached to this laptop. For believing in me and brainstorming with me when I got stuck. But most importantly, for loving me. I couldn't imagine my life without you in it. You make it revolve so perfectly. Thank you. For more than you know.

And finally, My Princesses, Madison-May and Ruby Rae. Thank you for giving me a purpose, for giving me a reason to be a better person and for teaching me about unconditional love. For brightening my world every morning with your smiles, and making my whole world so beautiful. Everything I do in life, my girls, I do it all for you. "I see who I want to be, in my daughters eyes"

Artwork by the incredibly talented-

Robert Alan Wallington.

Find him on Facebook:

'R.A.W TALENT ART'

Or email him at:

'RAW_TALENT81@YAHOO.CO.UK'

Lightning Source UK Ltd.
Milton Keynes UK
UKOW04f2130191217
314685UK00014BA/235/P